Warrior Winning Plan©

HIT THE TARGET VICTORY!

Step-By-Step Athletic Success

Jim Davis

Table of Contents

Dedication and Acknowledgments

The Warrior Winning Plan is dedicated to the late, Dr. Howard Hendricks (Dallas Seminary).

Dr. Hendricks personal, practical, confrontational teaching style called-out leaders and athletes to stand-up for their faith in God. His riveting-genius inspired my life and coaching.

Heartfelt gratitude to my loving, enthusiastic, supportive parents, Zelma and Dave Davis.

Special thanks to my coaches, mentors, family and friends for their amazing encouragement.

Deep appreciation to these organizations:

Bible.org© is a free, on-line commentary, highly-respected for insightful teachers, accuracy, context, clarity, and living-application.

Breakthrough Basketball ™ is your relevant, 'go-to' hoop website; complete with articulate instructors and helpful, educational videos.

About the Author

At 19 years old, my greatest love was gone…football. An All-State running back/linebacker at McLane High School in Fresno, California; five major injuries in four seasons not only shattered my body, but my psyche as well. After a 'season' of foolish choices and selfish, reckless behavior, I rededicated my life to God, and discovered real peace and a new perspective for athletics.

Enrolled at Fresno City College, I found myself in the library engrossed in Coach Magazine. In that quiet hall, I discovered the loud, missing pieces of my incomplete athletic experience. Years later, I took a Physical Education and coaching position at a small, private Christian school. Ironically, I published several articles for Coach Magazine. Armed with insight for improvement; I coached athletes from elementary age to college on the strategy and fundamentals missing in my career.

Philosophy in sport is greater than talent. Think of all the gifted athletes that never experience solid success. Why? They lacked innovative philosophy, principles and a plan for improvement. Insightful information is the green light driving the objectives of your goal – winning the prize! Visionary coaches sketch-out potential – inspiring players to paint the pictures of their dreams.

My short-term goal is to provide practical tips to help your performance improve immediately. My long-term goal is to share specific principles and clear steps to build a winning program. I cannot promise you winning, but I do offer a clear vision for victory. Athletic success organized! Warrior Winning Plan – Hit The Target Victory! Equipping giftedness to glorify God!

Jim Davis

Step-By-Step Athletic Success!

Problem: Dedicated athletes and coaches lack an innovative, step-by-step system for success. Solution: The Warrior Winning Plan is easy-to-read philosophy, principles, strategy and skills for insightful improvement, consistent high-level performance, intense competitiveness and fun. Four comprehensive steps train, equip, and prepare you to do what winning requires.

The plan offers a unique, winning mental approach for executing your giftedness under pressure. Special features include motivational-tips, leadership, and character that promote team-building.

Innovative, attacking systems for basketball, volleyball, and tennis are explained in clear details. Warrior-max Swing is a baseball/softball hitting system that 'connects' approach to success. 27 Reasons to Believe in the Fastball builds a solid foundation for successful pitching strategy. Basketball BEEFF Sharpshooter simplifies/unifies body positions for free throws and BIG shots.

The Warrior Winning Plan is faith-based athletic philosophy inspired with relevant Bible verses.

DAVID TOOK A RISK AND DEFEATED A GIANT!

DAVID

WARRIOR MODEL

- **Bold Faith**
- **Special Skill**
- **Unstoppable Game Plan**
- **Hit The Target Victory!**

1 Samuel: 17-18

Step One: Warrior Winning Fundamentals

100% Commitment - Motivation: Excitement for Reward!

Commitment: 100% dedication, whole-hearted connection to your goal.

Motivation: noble purpose and intense urgency in accomplishing the objectives of your goal.

Philosophy: principles stating your purpose and plan for accomplishing your goal.

Faith: going after your goal believing God will fulfill the passion in your soul.

Character: principle supersedes popularity; *I`m going to do the right thing!*

Angry Animal: mama bear protecting her cubs to eliminate a forcible threat.

Got Your Back Victory Vow: intense, personal, driving force not to let your teammates down.

Love for the Game and Glory: unbridled enthusiasm for your craft - playing for a championship!

Fresh Horses: optimism and energy for out-performing the competition! *I feel good!*

Team Motto: short, dynamic slogan expressing your competitive character. *Believe-Battle-WIN!*

Public Performance Epiphany: *I want to do that!* Immediate commitment to pursue a sport. Powerful identity incentive for a style that imitates your hero; participation in his brand.

Based on a Gusty, Glory Story: heroic, inspiring illustration for teambuilding and game readiness.

My Contribution: positive impact on a game from your input and innovation.

Deadline Consequences: accomplish assignments on time, or be dismissed from the program.

Over-Under-Around Challenge: creative persistence to break through a giant obstacle wall.

Fighting for Your Life: two strikes in the batter`s box. Goal-line-stand stubbornness - no Plan B. **Driven by Desperation:** overwhelming drive to defeat adversity, rescuing a teammate in trouble; saving your career by joining a successful program that matches your identity and special skill.

Tenacious Innovation: creative obsession to develop a revolutionary philosophy, superior weapon, unstoppable game plan, or a new practical, efficient system for performance success. Discover and explore an unknown frontier.

"I`m Sick of It!": conviction of truth; heartfelt confession to stop self-destructive behavior. Dramatic wake-up call providing positive fear, commitment and purpose for life-saving change.

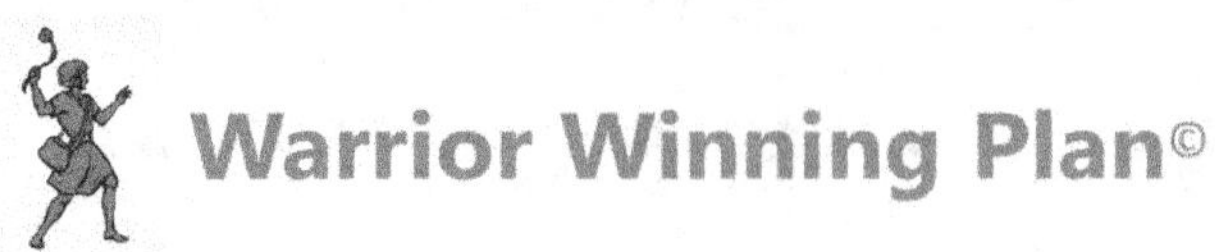

On a Mission for Pride and Position: chip on your shoulder to prove worth. Revenge for a loss; conquering your rival, restoring a program back to glory. Dedicating a game to a suffering teammate. Last chance for a personal goal - completing an important project for your legacy.

Single-minded Purpose: intentional knock-out blow to win the game!

Grind to find the Gold Mine: burning desire to discover and apply a performance 'nugget'.

Taking on the Treacherous Mountain: personal high-risk challenge for long-shot satisfaction.

Downhill Train Rolling: Success empowering success! Striking a spark that fires-up teammates! David defeating Goliath - contagious aggression for team progression!

Winning Motivating Winning!

Peaceful Focus – Winning Mental Approach

Peaceful Focus is a clear mind and a confident heart - a positive attitude for accomplishing goals. Peace is built on trust in God – allowing you to relax and establish rhythm in performance. Peaceful Focus locks into the picture in front of you - enhancing processing and recognition. Peaceful Focus 'opens-up' your senses (awareness) to perceive information for sound judgement. Peaceful Focus manages surprise adversity for a calm, consistent state of mind.

Peaceful Focus maintains patience and balance in executing fundamentals in BIG moments. Making contested basketball shots, connecting a swing to a deceptive rise-ball or an off-speed pitch, performing a variety of tennis strokes (on the move) requires a calm demeanor, soft hands and perfect timing for finesse shots and explosive follow-through in finishing plays.

Peaceful Focus provides mental toughness for the moment. Blocking-out disappointment is an effective tool in concentration, but humans are emotionally-based, reacting to failure with a wide array of analysis and feelings; including the 'let down' of not coming through for teammates.

Forgetting about missed opportunities requires mental discipline (easy to say - hard to do). Softball players make errors preoccupied with painful frustration from failed, hitting opportunities. Dropping your focus dulls the sharp, mental edge demanded for consistent, competitive performance. Trusting God for peace and perspective transitions distracting mistakes into readiness for the next play; Warriors do not allow mistakes to defeat them.

Peaceful Focus prevents burn-out; balancing pressure with perspective for positive performance. Peaceful Focus provides a sober mentality for serious issues like injuries and reckless violence. God`s peace protects the mind; He'll work-out your concern for the good, and His glory.

Adrenaline-aggression: working for you or against you? Athletes crave the power and euphoria of adrenaline-driven performance. Hyper-euphoria success puffs-up bravado making you believe you can do something you do not have the ability to do, and that's when mistakes happen.

Adrenaline-overload races the heart, scrambles thoughts, tightens muscles and diminishes power. Pitchers, quarterbacks, and tennis servers performing too 'high' or 'tight' struggle to hit their targets. Nerves disrupt timing, rhythm and confidence in execution - sabotaging best effort. Trying too hard is self-induced pressure creating 'over-play' mistakes.

Peaceful Focus balances emotion and effort, preventing flat-performance after BIG success. Efficiency = stamina. Maximum effort/minimum strain energizes fight at the end of-the-game.

- ▸ Worry is a hole in your energy bucket.
- ▸ Doubt is a thief – stealing belief.
- ▸ Distraction is a mental termite chewing away focus.
- ▸ Guilt is a troublemaker undermining confidence and decisiveness.
- ▸ Anger is a road-block for receiving information required for the challenge in front of you.
- ▸ Over-excitement is a flood of adrenaline producing mistakes that wash away opportunity.
- ▸ Self-consciousness (preoccupied with fear or guilt) restricts spontaneity in performance.

Butterfly-stress stimulates readiness for competition; worry frets about a future outcome. Performance-stress divides focus and emotional connection to your objective (winning). Pressure-stress rushes execution (getting ahead of the moment) when making a close play. Panic-stress freezes execution (tightening-up) causing game-changing mistakes in BIG moments. These examples of competitive stress are not clinical anxiety, but normal emotional reactions to game pressure. Crippling performance anxiety should be addressed by a sports psychologist.

High-stakes competition/reward produce tension and sloppy execution in championship games. Fear of losing intensifies pressure to win. Do not worry about winning the contest - focus on winning your assignment. Mental toughness executes skill and plays accurately under pressure. David took a daring risk and Hit The Target! Perform free of the fear of failure – embrace challenge with the certainty and competency of the Warrior Winning Plan. Don`t worry – trust God! Peaceful Focus releases emotional freedom for expressing giftedness in the moment.

Peaceful Focus is the psychological flow processing the competitive experience in front of you. Imagine driving your car on a steep, winding road in the mountains: concentrating on the road, visually locked into the lines, anticipating the next curve, mind and eyes directing hands and feet. Your fate lies in your focus, readiness and reactions to pass the test challenging your skill.

Awareness of God`s leadership in battle, builds belief in your competency to succeed in battle. David`s certainty for defeating Goliath was inspired from victories over vicious lions and bears. Power, passion, and sound judgement are God`s good gifts to your confidence and decisiveness. Feeling optimistic about opportunity makes competition fun!

Peaceful Focus Unlocks Your Victorious Spirit!

Fundamentals – Special Skill Hitting the Target!

Fundamentals are the basic skills required to perform a sport. Basic offensive fundamentals in basketball are the dribble, drive, jump-stop, pivot, cut, screen, pass, shot, block-out and rebound. Mechanics are the technical steps organizing proper body positions to execute fundamentals. Mechanics in BEEFF basketball shooting are balance, eyes, elbow, finger-tips, and follow-through. Basketball passing success: proper passing produces points and prevents transition play. Inaccurate passing creates rushed shots, sloppy play, and turnovers. Poor passing = poor results.

Fundamentals can be broken-down into two phases: prelaunch (foundation) and launch (finish). Volleyball prelaunch: ready position, eyes on the ball, call the ball, feet to the ball for platform. Launch: pass to setter, set for spike to space. Your finish is only as good as your foundation.

Study and imitate master athletes for insight at your position. Don`t let ignorance spoil potential. Lacking the knowledge and sophistication of your craft leads to failure, frustration, and quitting. Transitioning to higher competition demands deeper knowledge, expertise and a complete skill-set. Youth hitters learn to wait and adjust their swing to the curve ball for next-level challenge. Effective coaches match their players' progress with challenging competition.

Dedication, fundamentals and training lay the solid foundation for expressing your giftedness. Discipline liberates creativity. Creating music on a guitar requires chord mastery in your vocal key. Start with two chords that inspire a melody and let it grow; more chords equal more melody. Art, photography, and movies provide a refreshing break from competitive stress.

Success in sports is about controlling the competitive components that provide advantage. Fundamentals provide control of the body/ball for executing Special Skill in Hitting the Target! Special Skill (trained, high-level ability for a specific task) is forged in repetitive, situational drills. Unique moves position your Special Skill for a creative, scoring advantage on the court and field. Trained footwork equips lateral movement and change of direction to an angle, base, or space. Skill requires core strength, flexibility, explosiveness and hand-eye, foot-eye coordination. Improve balance and agility in navigating a safe, but challenging obstacle or ropes course.

Quick reflexes and timing coordinate body movements to connect a baseball swing to the pitch. Hitters struggle to make solid contact with the ball. Contact requires timing, strike identification, and swing adjustment. Timing is solved when the hitter gets-in-rhythm with the pitcher`s motion. Warrior-max swing: timing - pitcher raises arm into 'L' position, hitter lifts stride foot four inches off the ground to get-in-rhythm with the pitcher`s motion; identification – the hitter 'photographs' the ball out of the pitcher`s hand to identify a strike, stride foot intuitively comes down as the pitcher releases the ball; adjustment – the hitter adjusts his fast, flat swing to the pitch location. Pulling the outside pitch to the shortstop, or 'dropping your hands' under the ball (pitch plane) results in weak ground balls and pop-up outs. Stay balanced and trust your hands to finish your flat swing with explosive accuracy. Be aggressive but patient in RBI situations; make the pitcher throw you a hittable pitch. Key: adjust your swing to the pitch location.

Efficient pitch execution: think of your shoulder to your finger-tips as a swinging-lever-system delivering power and precision to your target with a smooth, wrist-snap and follow-through. Stretch and protect your remarkable hands and fingers. One serious injury can ruin your career.

Consistent high-performance starts with discipline and repetition in mastering fundamentals. Flawed fundamentals fracture physics. In basketball, BEEFF shooters position their shot in a straight line to the basket with their arm, hand and elbow directly over-the-hip (armpit level), fingertips are spread into the seams and the wrist is cocked-back for smooth, dynamic, release-rotation spin 'into the cookie jar.' Flaw: elbow drifts out of alignment from the shooting line.

Repetition of exact skill is difficult. Complex working parts in repetitive movement are manipulated by pressure, anxiety, doubt, distraction, adrenaline, tightness and fatigue. Depending on muscle memory in unorthodox skill produces flawed execution in game pressure. Peaceful Focus Fundamentals provide a safe, repeatable motion for precision in performance. Executing mechanics correctly requires balance in body positions, transitions and follow-through. Performance success: trusting your approach (strategies) and fundamentals under pressure. Maximizing technique and explosiveness accelerates improvement in your Special Skill.

Discipline trains with truth: coach fundamentals correctly and consistently with accountability. Be simple, clear and positive: don`t over-coach and confuse players with excessive information. Imperfect execution in practice results in flaws that frustrate and defeat you in the contest. Fundamentals minimize mistakes and maximize efficiency for your competitive advantage. Take pride in your fundamentals - practice them diligently every day and they will reward you.

Fundamentals Position Skill For Success!

Strong Identity – Unique Style & Strengths

Strong Identity is knowing who you are in God: faith, character, values, purpose and work-ethic. Unique Style is the creative expression of your personality, skills, strengths and performance. Strong Identity determines your approach to performance; compete out of that logical blueprint. Commit to coaches who provide opportunity and expertise to discover your identity and abilities. Does your style of play match your physicality, athleticism, and giftedness?

David knew who he was in God: a faithful, shepherd-warrior victorious in battling vicious beasts. Eliab, (David`s oldest brother) criticized David`s interest in the battle and motives for the victor`s reward as selfish immaturity. David ignored Eliab`s angry, verbal attack as baseless and invalid. He did not live to please his critics...David lived to please God. David knew his calling and purpose. God honored his faith and directed his fighting skills against the arrogant, loud-mouthed Goliath.

God will not call you to a mission without providing the will, talent and training to accomplish it. Do not let doubters diminish or discourage the dream God has burned deep into your heart. Dreams focus passion, purpose, talent, and objectives into a plan for accomplishing your goal. Nobody is going to knock on your door to fulfill your dream. Dreams are won on the battlefield! God will use your dream to inspire the dreams of others.

Study models for mind-set, training, drills, preparation, defeating adversity and competitiveness. Apply moves that match your athleticism. Integrate the steps of their technique into your style. Grow your future in the rich soil of yesterday`s heroes.

Tennis Styles – Player`s Coach – Identity Insights

Baseline Defender: fit, fast and agile; Power Aggressor: tall, strong with explosive winners. All-court: creative approach with multiple shots. Tennis players lacking a plan waste energy in rallies. Creating and finishing 'short balls' flow out of a smart strategy utilizing your Style & Strengths. Be flexible and adjust your approach to your opponent`s tactics without changing your style.

Positive coach identity: *I believe in you and your goals. I understand your success and failures. I enjoy coaching your character, talent, performance, and life-skills. I will always be here for you. When time tackles my body to the floor...strong arms will carry me on the court once more.*

Identity components: sex, name, birth place, relationships, personality, self-image, confidence, natural abilities, occupation, education, military service, community service and achievements.

Your personality expresses your Strong Identity. My first football coach was loud and demanding; testing my toughness in tackling drills and finishing long practices with exhausting wind sprints. Before a BIG game, he asked me if I was ready to play, I said, *yes!* and he replied, *you better be!*

Temperament and Personality Types

- Sanguine – Performer (personality plus!)
  Spontaneous, talkative, passionate, persuasive, theatrical, fun, life of the party.
- Choleric – Producer (problem-solver)
  Confident, intuitive, decisive, no-nonsense boss, goal-driven, visionary leader.
- Melancholic – Perfectionist (get-it-right mentality)
  Sensitive, sincere, self-sacrificing, analytical, gifted in organization, theory and creativity.
- Phlegmatic – Peace-keeper (get-the-facts before jumping into the fire)
  Calm, steady, competent in details, natural wit-humor, loyal friend, and patient listener.

Most people have two personality types with one temperament defining their identity. Temperament traits balance and complement each other for Strong Identity, Style & Strengths. Personality tests are available through career counselors to help you discover your temperament. Patience, experience and social interactions will help you apply your traits to your performance.

Understanding personality strengths/weaknesses provides flexibility and unity in relationships. Understanding temperament traits prevents over-reacting to irritating, annoying behavior. Understanding temperament strengths enhances recognition for roles in leadership and service.

Be yourself and express your personality, but be aware of verbal triggers like teasing, insults, angry outbursts, complaining and arguing that sabotage sportsmanship and Peaceful Focus. Disrespecting your opponent with antagonistic talk motivates/energizes his effort against you.

Expressing honest feelings appropriately allows you to take a stand for your concerns and values. People lacking courage and tact to express their opinions become passive-aggressive victims. Be true to your identity in God. Creating a popular image to please people restricts self-expression.

God gifted Adam in the Garden of Eden with the imagination/verbal skills to name the animals. God has gifted you with the ability to perform a specific role at a high-level with confidence. Success enriches and expands your confidence and Strong Identity for a greater responsibility. Opportunity for new adventure and challenge is like an inspiring, panoramic ocean view; providing wider perspective for possibility and a deeper dive into the discovery of new waters.

Before the game, create an action highlight reel in your imagination of the winning outcome. Step into the facility and take-in the panoramic view of the field, arena, or stadium...visualize your performance. See yourself executing your Special Skill, making exciting plays and having fun! Feel the satisfaction of celebrating success with teammates, family and friends...GO FOR IT!!!

Frustration in losing can cause hot, hateful, ugly emotions to boil over into violent behavior. Frustration penalties hurt the team, diminish your character and positive impact on the game. Losing is capital; an investment into your next win. Failure is opportunity to figure-out success. Improvement: losing to a superior team can be more productive than beating an inferior team. A painful loss today, can propel your program into completeness for a championship tomorrow.

Evaluate what component of the game plan failed? What caused the failure? How can I fix it? What specific mistakes impacted the loss? Was I mentally and physically prepared to compete? Did foolish, selfish choices the night before the game diminish my focus, energy and will to win? Did I apply my practice priorities in the game? Did I underestimate my opponent's firepower? Did my opponent play with more toughness? Did I adjust to my opponent's strategy and tactics? Did my opponent outperform me in BIG moments? What is one major takeaway from this loss?

Basing your self-worth on roller-coaster sports performance creates unreasonable expectations. Perfect perspective vs perfect performance: human factor reality - people make mistakes. Authentic self-worth is found in faith in God. True reward is experiencing His unconditional love. God will develop and bless your passion; it's not what you do, but rather Who is living in you.

Winning is a huge challenge. Taking total control of the game 'for the win' is simplistic thinking. Controlling your actions is a winning testimony of your Strong Identity and sportsmanship.

Knowing Who You Are In God - Provides Power For The Job!

Alpha Vocal Leaders – Victorious Spirit!

Alpha Vocal Leaders do what is best for the team. They take charge to establish momentum. Basketball pass-first guards set their teammates up for scoring, but also score when necessary. Alpha Vocal Leaders expect unselfish play; they address teammates disrupting team objectives. When losing, Alpha Vocal Leaders rally teammates to unite and fight for a comeback victory! Alpha Vocal Leaders love tough competition - the higher the stakes...the better they play!

Alpha Vocal Leaders are straightforward in communication; investing in authentic relationships. Alpha Vocal Leaders are trustworthy: dependable in service - demonstrating loyalty to culture. Alpha Vocal Leaders come to practice 'on a mission' equipped with serious, intentional focus. Alpha Vocal Leaders execute drills with energy and excellence; calling-out distracted teammates. Teammates emulate their leader's attitude and actions.

Players respect coaches with leadership, bold vision, organization, innovation and motivation. Athletes commit to winning programs with integrity, career-vision, and a family atmosphere. Authentic coaches win trust and loyalty through communication, consistency and shared success. Teams reflect their coach's identity, character, courage, work-ethic and approach to life.

Effective mentors provide insightful counseling for connecting-the-dots of success in education. Pushing players to make correct choices on their path for maturity and adulthood is top priority. Wise mentors encourage players to share their stories, knowledge, disappointments and success. Players willing to be mentored become confident, decisive problem-solvers.

Alpha Vocal Leaders Inspire Championship Play!

Unstoppable Game Plan – Playing Ahead of Your Opponent

Plan your attack. Work-out details of execution. Practice, refine and perfect your attack. Executing your plan efficiently requires situational practice. Do not get discouraged – persist! Game Plan: objectives to be accomplished. Strategy: how objectives will be accomplished. Advancement: applying strategy to opportunity – using skills/weapons to accomplish objectives. Opportunity knocks: choose the best tactics for high percentage success. Target weakness! Establish momentum with correct decisions, rhythm and efficiency. Use creativity to score!

Innovation: a new practical, efficient system for accurate application of solution to problem. 1960s UCLA Men`s Basketball innovated a full-court-press to break Cal Bears` dominance. Disrupting your opponent`s rhythm and establishing your rhythm creates a scoring advantage.

Wolfpack attack is relentless: stop your opponent`s advancement with a powerful wall of force, pin down his position - finish your mighty mission. Anticipate his tactics and control his weapons. "Strike-the-shepherd": double-teaming the 'shepherd' drains his physical and emotional energy; pressing teammates into uncomfortable roles attempting to make scoring plays in high pressure. Superstars, forcing ill-advised moves (to prove their greatness) become their own defenders.

New approach – better result: consistently losing to an evenly matched opponent in talent, teamwork and toughness signals your opponent has figured out your offense and defense. Counter your opponent`s tactics with a new, creative strategy and weapons difficult to defend. Perceptive court/field management keeps your adjustments ahead of your opponent`s attack.

Knowing how to win, creates confidence to win! Example: 3DFlash Attack Basketball. Overload the court (strong side to weak side attack) – pass to flasher cutting-off the screen, **Drive** to the paint, **Draw** the defender and **Dish** to roller/cutter. Knowledge unlocks victory`s door!

David, a brave teen-shepherd, honed his fighting skills protecting his sheep from lions and bears. His superior air attack defeated Goliath`s ground attack. Focus on the plan – Hit the Target!

Alert anticipation advantage: ability to visualize and recognize your opponent`s next move. Knowing your opponent`s tendencies in specific situations creates opportunity for special plays. Counter your opponent`s substitutions with specific plays exploiting one-on-one mismatches. Halftime assessment: identify specific issues – provide steps and details for solutions. Be positive!

Script a series of creative plays to establish timing, rhythm and confidence for a successful start. Apply a quick pace to keep your opponent back-on-his-heels for the surprise, knockout blow. Create and take advantage of opportunity: successful plays set up successful plays. The rushing attack in football sets-up play-action passing. Defense in basketball produces fastbreak scoring.

Innovation is an efficient system for applying the correct application of solution to the problem. Football games are won with a successful strategy for fielding punts on a muddy, slippery field. Bill Walsh (1980s SF Football) forced linebackers to cover speedy backs on quick pass routes. Softball games are won with surprise bunting and bold, late-inning baserunning tactics.

Study your opponent's style, system, sets, strategy, strengths and the star's inclinations. Perceive patterns, body language, dominate side of court, and the go-to-player in big moments. Recognize specific, situational plays. Identify the time your opponent 'hits the wall' of fatigue. Neutralize strength - take away options – exploit weakness. Isolate mismatches for direct attack. Identify specific areas of the court or field that your opponent is not guarding, or cannot defend.

Your Unstoppable Game Plan should incorporate all your weapons to overwhelm your opponent. The best teams use the best players in the best ways to win. Take advantage of opportunities in specific situations to execute your players' Special Skills. Establishing one player's Special Skill opens-up opportunity for another player's Special Skill. An explosive base stealer creates high fastballs for a home-run hitter. A three-point shooter opens-up the key for a scoring center.

Lack of success creates the blame game. The coach criticizes players lack of effort and execution. Frustrated players criticize the coach's ability to game plan/use weapons - morale 'hits the wall.' The Warrior Winning Plan will invigorate the team and restore optimism.

Develop a physicality to control and dominate the high-percentage, scoring zone in the game. Tennis players control the baseline by powering the ball into the corners to create short balls. Basketball players control the key for disrupting lay-ups and making easy, high-percentage shots. Football linemen control the line-of-scrimmage for running, passing/receiving opportunities. Volleyball players control the net for blocking and spiking advantages. Pitchers control the plate.

Baseball pitching plan: hit your spots with control, movement, speed/off-speed and pitch variety. Pitch ahead in the count, keep the hitter off-balance, visualize and anticipate the next swing. Throw the illusion of a strike for your 'out' pitch: off-speed below-the-zone, curve and slider outside-the-zone, two-seamer or backfoot slider inside-the-zone and fastball above-the-zone.

Set-up hitters: exploit their weaknesses – dropping the hands, loopy swing, hole-in-the swing, poor swing adjustment to pitch location, first pitch swinging, slow bat-speed, lack of discipline for high-fastball, trouble with the curve, poor plate coverage, lunging at off-speed, backfoot slider blind-spot, over-aggressive swinging in RBI situations, 'freezes' on low-inside third strike fastball, and strikes out in home run greed. Third strike 'out' pitch: execute the pitch in an unhittable spot.

Pitching strategy: establish lower outside-half of the plate with four and two-seam fastballs, sinker, slider and curve ball. Pitch inside (under-the-hands) with two-seam fastball, sinker, slider, off-speed. Pitch inside (over-the-hands) with four-seamer. No mistakes over the plate!

Left-handed hitters pull low-inside pitches for home runs. Right-handed hitters attack high pitches over-the-plate for home-runs. Counter the upper-cut (home run swing), with off-speed below the zone, or a 'rising' fastball above-the-zone. Pitcher's kryptonite: lead-off walks!

First inning: connect with the umpire's strike zone. Low-ball law: *low you roll...high you cry.* Remember, pitching is nine defenders against one hitter. Be patient, do not rush your mechanics! You make smart pitches – the defense makes great plays.

Track and Field competitors assert their Special Skill into the competition for a unique advantage. They utilize Peaceful Focus and a winning plan to execute speed, strength, talent, technique, and greatness into a strong, explosive finish! Winners do what winning requires!

The Warrior Winning Plan provides success steps for soccer, field hockey, and all other sports. Athletic Success Organized!

A Faithful Man Executes The Game Plan!

Clear & Attack Space – Create Open Targets

Athleticism does not guarantee success: creative tactics and bold, timely-skill creates success. Knowledge breaks down your opponent's defense and shuts down your opponent's offense. Creativity connects purpose to play: it clears and attacks space for efficient offense (deception). Creativity attacks and takes away space for pressure defense (disruption).

Smart, fast, defensive players cover the court (Attacking/Taking Away Space) to prevent scoring. Clearing space opens-up the court to locate the ball in a place your opponent cannot defend. Understanding creative space tactics allows you to adjust and break down different defenses. Clearing/Attacking space is unpredictable, balanced, and not dependent upon the star for scoring. You have the talent and toughness – do you possess the creativity and courage to win the contest?

Clearing space allows pass receivers to get open and running backs to burst through the hole. Establishing a quarterback pocket provides time for receivers to create space for another receiver. Attacking to Take Away Space (blitzing) disrupts the quarterback's timing to throw the pass.

Risk-reward: an explosive, well-timed, creative offense quickly separates the score in your favor. Top teams know and execute each other's plays; evenly matched games are won with creativity. Be bold and decisive; take advantage of a scoring window before the opportunity shuts down. Lack of offense deflates defense – successful offense energizes defense.

Like eagle glory gliding through the sky – creative scoring is a soaring high!

Creative Success Motivates More Success!

In-Sync Teamwork – One Mighty Force!

In-Sync Teamwork is the perfect storm of a plan, purpose, and passion complementing and completing one another's abilities. It combines communication and cooperation in competition. Teamwork starts in positive relationships; chemistry is the rocket fuel powering champions!

Accountability calls-out teammates to transparency. Members hold each other responsible for safe, personal/public activities that protect the health, well-being and high character of the team. T.E.A.M: Trust, Encourage, Assist, Master responsibilities. Follow T.E.A.M. leaders.

Honor your commitments: respond to requests for help with an enthusiastic 'can do' attitude. Your energy and talent provide an extra set of hands to push the task across the finish line. Teammates connected in service receive an A in 'chemistry' class.

Timing is the key for executing efficient plays; it prevents the defense from taking away space. Synergy (team interaction): executing your role enables teammates to execute their roles. Chemistry in chaos: staying poised as One Mighty Force improvising and problem-solving.

Winning requires a team effort with effective execution in all phases of offense and defense. Trust your teammates' motives; value their input, talents, and contributions. Faithfulness unites a team to play well together in finding ways to win.

The human body has many parts with different abilities working In-Sync to accomplish a goal. Team body: equal in value, different in roles - one in purpose. Powerful legs need humble feet! Team firepower: weapons working in unity as One Mighty Force!

Your teeth are locked into your gums as a team. Top teeth complementing bottom teeth in design, partnership and purpose - working together to release flavor and energy for the body.

The hand consists of five fingers with each one having a specific function. The receiving corps in football has five receivers, each with a specific role for running pass routes. Thumb: Tight End– strong x-factor. Index: Slot- quick mismatch on linebackers. Middle: Power- big, versatile and unstoppable. Ring: Possession- finds space for first downs. Pinky: Wide- small, shifty, explosive!

Effective coaches equip players with tools for competency and completeness in competition. Expertise develops special skills and confidence for God-given (natural) athletic ability/instincts. A positive attitude and Special Skill integrate your role into the body of the team.

Use your Special Skill to maximize your teammates` Special Skills. Creative volleyball setters locate the ball at unpredictable spots along the net - providing vision for hitters to attack space.

Dynamic-depth factor: role players providing energy and firepower to finish-off fatigued teams. Sweet Success: talent & timing producing power & precision with cool execution in hot sweat. Discipline and sacrifice in due diligence is overwhelmed and forgotten in BIG victory celebration! Elite players perform at elite levels when they feel the trust and support of their teammates. The goal to do what winning requires is emboldened in team-first camaraderie.

Championship teams are complete teams with bold, innovative leadership, versatile talent, and bench depth; unified and committed to defeat adversity in accomplishing an extraordinary goal. Game-changing plays are made with belief and execution in spontaneous team agility.

Stay grounded in humility on victory mountain. Disappointment can be devastating to a BIG ego. One moment you are standing in sunshine of success - next moment free-falling in dark failure. Victory celebration is a two-edged sword; burning fuel tonight leaves your tank empty tomorrow. An over-high opinion of your ability causes you to underestimate your opponent`s ability. Underestimating your opponent`s ability leaves you flatfooted and frustrated lacking firepower.

E-factor in Excellence: Enthusiasm – Energy – Effort - Efficiency – Effectiveness – Endurance!

Locker Room Blueprint: foundation of commitment, encouraging walls of support, character roof of protection and decorated with inspirational mottos; *yesterday`s glory inspiring victory today!* Improve for each other. Team growth requires every member to maximize his God-given talent. There is no room for jealousy in a happy house - celebrate family success!

Resolve disagreements with good-will, communication, and compromise for a common goal. Protect team privacy: agree on team values publicly - disagree on personal opinions privately. The best air-freshener is fresh air.

Master your job description with enthusiasm! Be an improvement beast hungry for fresh meat! Enthusiasm is free - apply it liberally!

Loyalty is a sacred agreement to honor, sacrifice, and serve your teammates on the battlefield. Are you energetic and ready to compete? Do you stay positive when the score is negative? Do you lift teammates up when your game performance goes down? Do you criticize or energize? Does your attitude, energy and effort match your 100% verbal commitment to the team?

Teamwork is athletic art in action. Sacrificing personal success for team success is true success! Two gifts are better than one gift: complementary special skills executing high-level performance. Your best memories will be the close camaraderie in the trenches overcoming giant obstacles.

Winning Connections: knowledge & confidence; motivation & effort; discipline & training; conditioning & fitness; passion & talent; learning & development; cooperation & leadership; chemistry & teamwork; precision & execution; skill & scoring; will & winning; success & goal! Honesty is the heart of humility – honor your teammates in your success!

Six broken-play mistakes: mental error (lack of focus), stress (distracted and pre-occupied), missed assignment, weak effort, poor technique, and failure to counter opponent's tactics. Staying organized and playing under control minimizes mistakes and maximizes productivity. Making adjustments = success. Executing your assignment requires a perceptive mind, nimble feet, and strong, coordinated hands to adjust to the evolving challenge in front of you.

Little details are a BIG deal in team skill. Humility desires direction – arrogance curses correction. Tree-trimming approach for growth: prune dead branches to direct energy into healthy branches. 100% commitment for a winning season: single-minded focus for turning weakness into strength. Your teamwork goal: efficiency! Fast, accurate high performance. Athletic success organized!

Be an inspiring player that makes plays and fires-up teammates when you are behind in the score. Come off the bench with confidence, ready to impact the game with hustle and Special Skill. Steadfastness is the fabric of faith holding struggling teams together in the season of storms. Unifying mind, body and spirit into one team ignites focus, smart decisions and great plays!

Teamwork: The Highest Skill And Biggest Thrill In All Of Sport!

Communication Executing Organization

Communicating specific issues with clarity and intensity facilitates adjustments in the game. Communication between coach and player provides same-page approach; player input enhances ownership. Raining ideas (brainstorming): requesting input floods the challenge with options. Collaboration energizes innovation; group discussion spurs spontaneous problem-solving. Another set of eyes may identify an unseen issue, or a new approach to an old issue.

Recognizing negative, non-verbal communication and body language may reveal a conflict. Stay connected to your team: reasoning together in a spirit of fairness solves serious issues. Conflict is a natural component in healthy relationships. Problem-solving is an imperative skill. Disagreeing without personal attack promotes openness and self-disclosure for both parties. Address the problem, identify the cause, solve with compromise, creativity, and common sense. Honest communication is the muscle in strong relationships.

God`s still, quiet voice calls for action for your good and His glory; pursue His counsel. God is God, he will always do what is best for you. His Word is the sacred standard for your life-decisions. Sacred moment in God`s presence: deep, spiritual focus and communication over a serious issue.

Peeling the onion: post-game self-analysis/anxiety over mistakes steals the thrill of the contest. Reliving and rehashing your mistakes alone invites stress, destructive behavior and insomnia. Disclose concerns with a trusted teammate. Sharing your real self...puts the game on the shelf.

Sharing meals, stories of outdoor adventures, surprising experiences, and insights of common subjects and hobbies opens-up free-flowing communication for a deeper bond with teammates. Be the most positive person in the room. Teambuilding ignites in a sincere, personal greeting. Look your coaches/teammates in the eye, acknowledge their name/presence with enthusiasm! You never know how a teammate is feeling - encouragement lifts-up wavering confidence.

Communication facilitates relationships for problem-solving, peace of mind and harmony. Authentic teammates are engaged listeners expressing genuine interest with open-ended questions; i.e. *How did the meeting go with Coach?* Lively two-way communication is like playing catch with a football. Your teammate passes information for you to receive and pass back with understanding. Constant interrupting, or pretending to listen is dropping the ball. Eye contact, responsive feedback, humor, and relevant insights are touchdowns! Problem-solving partners listen intently for clarification: the speaker shares thoughts and feelings about a confusing issue, the listener gives insightful feedback helping the speaker clarify the issue and solve the problem.

Feelings express deep emotions as important reminders to take immediate action for an issue. Angry, bitter feelings draw attention to a personal problem affecting your attitude/best effort. Mature teammates communicate feelings with facts and tact to protect unity and team morale. Uplifting feelings spark awareness and appreciation for mentors, memories, and milestones.

Inventory your true emotional condition; hidden, unresolved issues sabotage performance. Disappointment is like a barbell on your neck. Take the weight off...talk to a caring counselor. Self-disclosure, removes the *I'm strong and successful* public mask, for an honest, personal, inside look at painful, festering issues. Tell your story: lives are changed when courage is shared. Friendships connect in communication and deepen in shared perspectives in tough trials.

Beauty is birthed at the bottom of a broken heart. Sharing the healing of your emotional pain, helps others in emotional pain to stop recycling destructive behavior into shame. Psychosomatic pain: repressing anxiety is the worst thing – expressing anxiety is the best thing. Sharing with a trusted friend transitions worry for the future into peace for the day.

Busy coaches, don't forget about your team at home waiting patiently for your leadership, guidance and encouragement. Showing-up means being there for your family, helping them understand and navigate their life-experiences. Family teamwork: hearts connected in love, serving one another with appreciation and joy. As a caring provider be generous with hugs and stingy with criticism. Invest in what you love and love what you invest in - your precious family.

The friendly bird invited a young bug to come over to his house for a spring dinner. The termite replied: *I've been eating at your house all winter.* Gossip destroys teams from the inside-out.

Artificial intelligence memorizes a million images to recognize one health issue. Film sessions and situational practices built on repetition and communication identify details for recognition.

Communication is not a murky green pond - it's a crystal blue river of ideas.

Accurate Information Organizes A Winning Plan!

Halftime Effort Assessment

- Vanilla: lack of purpose, urgency and hustle.

- Red: poor execution from performance stress.

- Gray: drop in focus, taking the pedal off the metal.

- Yellow: giving-up in adversity.

- Black: fighting back!

- Green: energetic, efficient execution!

- Blue: in-the-zone high performance!

- Purple: elite, amazing play!

You Will Never Be A Champion Playing Afraid.

Be Bold – Take A Reasonable Risk For A Worthy Reward!

Extra Gear of Greatness

Extra Gear of Greatness: unique, creative ability consistently performed at an elite level!

Execution Zone: precision, firepower and dominance in competition!

Adrenaline Zone: superman soaring in crowd-pleasing excitement!

Skill-At-Will Zone: instinctual agility and instant ability to get the job done!

Easy Zone: fun, fearless, flowing execution!

Power Zone: explosive impact on the game!

Greatness Zone: transitioning giftedness into greatness to make winning plays!

Creative Zone: unique signature moves in BIG Moments!

Sacrifice Zone: performance forged in pain - polished in patience - completed in persistence!

Babe Ruth's famous home runs started with quick perception for identifying a hittable pitch. Gifted with bold belief, he had the agility to adjust his explosive flat swing to the pitch location. Gale Sayers, (NFL running back) improvised, elusive runs with gifted feet, stop-n-go acceleration, peripheral vision, horizontal cuts, tackle-breaking balance and touchdown-blasting speed!

Great players are not content with breaking records, media accolades, and superhero worship. They are hungry competitors obsessed with one priority: improve today – play better tomorrow! Their true motivation is passion for the game - not to impress others with their talent and fame. Disciplined habits position players at the right place/right time to take advantage of opportunity.

Greatness just keeps getting better: Nolan Ryan pitched his seventh no-hitter at 44 years old. Fitness, fundamentals and firepower to finish-off hitters were the key to his unique longevity. Good players are good most of the time - great players are great all of the time. Willie Mays' baseball genius and natural ability defied limitations - celebrating greatness with passion, hustle, and spectacular plays. Willie was my model, inspiration and first athletic hero.

Maximizing giftedness: challenge yourself to discover/develop all your weapons (Special Skills). The more weapons you develop...the more versatility you offer your team for creative attack. Volunteer to serve at events for winning programs. Great organizations model successful culture.

Discovering a rich, mountain range of community greatness is high adventure in coaching. Your legacy as a coach will be identifying your players` gifts and impacting their character. Winning truth: good coaches preach winning - great coaches teach what winning requires.

Great competitors are not complacent with their strong performance in early game success. Focused on their objective and wanting more - their rhythm roars like waves pounding the shore. Great performers thrive in championship play. Perceiving unseen possibility; they rise up with courage, elite skill and breath-taking artistry to stun and dismantle their opponent`s attack. Dominators perceive quickly, executing elite skill with power and precision.

Building their body-of-work through consistent winning - champions are poised in BIG contests. The higher you move-up the 'food chain' of tough competition - the more your flaws are exposed. Bold competitors are motivated by a cunning opponent attacking a perceived weakness.

Inspiring coaches are enthusiastic teambuilders: authentic, intentional, caring mentors who educate their team in the rich history, heroes, identity, social impact and legacy of their sport. Committed to sound, conventional tactics; they are open-minded to new, successful trends. Balancing control with trust they delegate creative responsibilities to talented, assistant coaches. Great coaches not only build confidence and win games, they win a generation of positive lives.

Bobby Bowden (Florida State Football) turned painful losses into two national championships. A bold, caring coach; he fought for his players off the field and they fought for him on the field. Coach Bowden, a risk-taker with 'go-for-it' belief innovated explosive scoring in BIG moments! Visionary coaches sketch-out potential...inspiring players to paint the pictures of their dreams.

Elevate Your Performance In God`s Strength!

Fight & Finish Strong!

Commit 100% to your goal...stomp on the gas and go! Warriors Fight and Finish Strong!
Peaceful Focus does not panic over mistakes. Setbacks will shake you, don`t let them break you.
Fear of finishing chokes opportunity with unforced errors. Faith in finishing makes BIG plays!

Resolve: strong-minded, refusing to back away from the challenge.

Extra effort: the deeper you dig...the more you give.

Toughness in the trenches: no retreat in these feet.

Fierceness: tenacious action for victory satisfaction.

Fight: main component to outperform your opponent.

Playing hard: aggression without concession.

Hustle: beating your opponent to the ball, base, and space.

Team Strength: the ultimate source for One Mighty Force!

Honest competitor questions: am I outsmarting, outperforming and outscoring my opponent?
Competition intrigue with drama driving the surprise of sport...who will sing the victory song?
Comeback victory in adversity - with courage and skill you fought and finished strong!

Your performance goal is to be a complete competitor who knows how to finish-the-fight.
Champions build their 'performance house' on the Warrior Winning Plan Foundation.

Tournament wins propel you into the night - energy provides fireworks for winning the fight!
There is no substitute for spirited subs; a strong, spirited bench is the backbone of the team.

Resilience: the muscle in persistence to fight on! Resolve: the grip of tenacity to fight long!
Distance runner courage: the stubborn persistence to fulfill the sacrifices required of winning.
Train, discipline and push your body in work-outs. Alpha leaders finish strong in wind sprints.
Like a racehorse powering through space and time, stamina will roll you across the finish line!

Mental toughness is the reward of intense battle against motivated rivals. You`re only as tough
as the adversity you`ve been through. David slayed lions and bears before he defeated Goliath.
X-factor: your body-of-work battling tough opponents shapes your competitive character.

The Wolverine is a small, but tenacious fighter with amazing traits: fast, powerful, agile,
cunning, stubborn and relentless. Exploiting every animal`s fear of injury, his up-close attack
forces his opponent to put 'skin in the game.' The Wolverine simply outfights his opponent.
Never back down in the battle - compete like a Wolverine!

Joy is your secret weapon for staying strong in set-backs. Like muscle energizes physical strength, joy energizes mental strength to embrace trials as tools for toughness, learning, and persistence. Persistence powers past pain and problems to accomplish its noble purpose. Believe-Battle-WIN!

Finish The Fight With Honor!

Hit the Target Performance - Bold Belief for Victory!

Noble motivation: David, strong-minded and full of faith, took a dangerous risk for his country. Only a teenage shepherd, he knew God would fight for him against the ten-foot, armored Goliath!

Initiate advantage: David sprinted to Goliath to establish the exact distance for his air attack.

Unstoppable Game Plan: utilize a strategy and superior weapon your opponent cannot defend.

Game management: make smart moves to counter and stay ahead of your opponent's attack.

Alert pressure defense: attack and take away space. Shut down your opponent's main weapon. Know your opponent's tendencies: be in the right place to disrupt timing and rhythm of the play.

First-strike aggression: establish success and confidence with correct decisions and efficient play. Tactics create opportunity. Disabling beasts with his sling gave David a competitive advantage. His air attack versus Goliath's ground attack would strike a critical, first blow from a distance.

Execute your giftedness: assert your will and Special Skill, outhustle/outperform your opponent! Consistent high-level play pressures opponent's into failure, frustration and giving-up the fight. David expressed his Strong Identity, executing his sling and stone-attack with accurate firepower.

Inject vertigo to create an open target: Clear & Attack Space with deception and Special Skill. David appeared weak and defenseless. He distracted Goliath with a stick, and then surprised him with an explosive, stone penetrating deep into Goliath's forehead. David Hit The Target!

Match your opponent's moves: counter his offensive excellence with your defensive excellence. Keep your opponent off-balance with fast, innovative tactics that take away his response time.

Fear of failure/distraction: getting ahead of the moment (rushing execution) causes mistakes. Apply solid fundamentals; see and secure the ball into your hands before you run with it.

Referees are not your opponent: don't fret and get upset about a bad call out of your control. Painful mistakes eat-up distracted teams - don't let the pity piranha devour your dream!

Assuming victory is defeat: expect your opponent to unleash overwhelming will and firepower! Anticipate his weapons - answer his aggression. Change your course with new tactics of force.

Organized offense advantage: In-Sync Teamwork is more productive than individual effort. Forcing ill-advised plays into tight areas produces turnovers. Relax and recognize shots to space. Locate the ball in a place fast defenders cannot defend. Be smart - pick your opponent apart!

Make the most of the moment: use savvy and instincts to create surprise and pressure situations. Make the right decision to gain strong position. Take advantage of mistakes with decisiveness.

Warrior Winning Plan©

High expectation - frustrating result: negotiate disappointment with positive perspective. Minimize distraction to stay in the action. Peace prevents the present from a war with the past. Forget failure. Trust and focus on the next play in front of you. Success rewards readiness!

Adapt to adversity with quick thinking and common sense: recognize and address issues. Problems are solved with nimble thinking and creative persistence. Your success is one idea away.

Collaborate for new strategies: consult teammates to discover and exploit hidden opportunities. Observe body language for tipping-off plays, patterns, surprise tactics, fatigue, and quitting.

Super-Hero Kryptonite: don't let one super-talented competitor control the pace of the game. Double-down and disrupt in-the-zone dominance. Maintain positive body language and self-talk.

Hustle wins opportunity: move quickly to beat your opponent to the ball, the base, and space! Feel the tiger's roar as he paces the floor! Ignite your passion! Release your Victorious Spirit!

Stubborn-Strong: stay strong when your opponent is on a 'run.' Your system is your strength.

When your opponent is down – don't let him hang around: David hustled to complete the job. Perceive weakness and finish-off fatigue - don't let a second wind help him believe.

Value momentum: maintain your competitive advantage - eliminate high-risk, impulsive plays. Do not play it safe, play to win and not to lose. Take a reasonable risk for a worthy reward!

Championship Leadership: vocal leaders inspire teammates to step-up and make BIG plays!

Super-success folly: temper hyper-euphoria, ego-inflation, reckless anger and foolish choices. Submit emotion to sound judgement. Restraint reveals character.

Playing well together requires consistent focus: do not be fooled by the illusion of early success. Taking the pedal-off-the-metal (complacency) knocks your rhythm out-of-gear into sloppy play. Do not play the blame game - regain the flow of your A-game!

Time is ticking: do not waste time when you're behind...hustle! Make a BIG play to save the day!

Quick response: recognize the threat - anticipate the pattern of attack - disable the weapon. Neutralize your opponent's effective strategy by applying his own tactics against him.

Competitive character: winners do what winning requires - execute all phases of your attack. Utilize all weapons on the entire field - be complete. Stick to the game plan...feed the hot hand!

Resiliency: your opponent's success will be your greatest test. Take the hit/fight back with grit. Failure injects doubt into skill - trust, focus and reset your will. Perseverance crowns the victor!

When plans and performance fall short: losers look for excuses – winners seek solutions.

Digging-out-of-the-hole: throw dirt on giving-up and get muddy executing one-play-at-a time. Make sure all phases of your team effort are executing their responsibilities correctly. BELIEVE!

Winning requires great plays: the close contest is calling for your Extra Gear of Greatness!

Peaceful Focus in crunch time: build a bridge of trust to overcome choking in BIG moments. As success increases - fear of failure decreases. March forward in optimism expecting success!

Tenacity and toughness: look the giant challenge 'in-the-eye' with single-minded persistence. Like a fisherman reeling in his stubborn catch - the grip on your goal burns fierce in your soul. Perseverance crowns the victor!

Relentless attack earns the victory: exert strength - exploit weakness - dominate mismatches. Control the pace to lead the race. Take charge! Fight & Finish Strong with your knock-out blow!

Find ways to win: stay alert, aggressive and organized through the finish line…don't let up! Capitalize on experience. Utilize surprise at the right time. Make BIG plays for the BIG ending!

Two-edged sword pain: burning excess fuel tonight – empties your tank for tomorrow. Celebrate victory! Move on and disconnect from your adrenaline-high. Relax and go to bed.

Evaluate (ASAP) – improve your craft: what specific adjustment defeated adversity for the win? How did you respond to emotional challenges, injuries, disappointments or poor officiating? Celebrate one skill/tactic you improved on!

Competitive Character - Your Key To Victory!

Step Two: Faith Principles for Winning

Warrior Winning Plan©

Faith - Vision the Eye Cannot See

(Biblical Insights)

Faith is being sure God exists and convinced all His promises are true. (Hebrews 11:1)

Ask God for peace to minimize stress and maximize confidence in your performance. (1 Peter 5:7)

Obey God`s command for bravery - trust His presence for success. (Joshua 1:9)

God`s Word inspires vision and boldness for great achievement. (Hebrews 11)

When confronted by fear; God empowers faith with passion and discipline. (2 Timothy 1:7)

Attack impossibility with God`s possibility! (Matthew 19:26)

Belief in God builds belief in yourself. Compete in His strength! (Philippians 4:13)

God fights for you! Goliath`s faith was in his sword. David`s faith was in the Lord! (1 Samuel 17:37)

Commit your goal to God. He will direct your plans and objectives. (Proverbs 16:3)

God`s heart and purpose is to bless your life with His success. (Jeremiah 29:11)

God gifted you to help and encourage others. (Ephesians 4:12)

Expressing your giftedness glorifies God. (Matthew 5:16)

God blesses skill with honor. (Proverbs 22:29)

Forget past mistakes and focus on future victory. (Philippians 3:13,14)

Holding on to the last knot on God`s rope stretches your faith. (Exodus 6:6) (James 1:2-4)

Ask God for wisdom and perspective for your trial. (James 1:5)

Watch God work-out the details of your dream. Celebrate His perfect gifts! (James 1:17)

Win the prize...run smart with all your heart! (1 Corinthians 9:24, Colossians 3:23)

In faith, request God`s help with anxious issues. His peace will protect your mind and emotions. Meditate on inspiring ideas – imitate the bold actions of biblical Warriors! (Philippians 4:4-9)

God`s command for action: Hear the Word...do the Word! (James 1:22)

Truth Topples Giants!

Step Three: Character Expressing Faith

High Character Sportsmanship

Remodel your tired thinking…build a library of noble thoughts.

High Character honors people and boundaries with respect, honesty, fairness and courtesy.

Principle supersedes popularity; base your decisions on facts and context…not on pleasing others.

Your private walk must match your public talk.

Decisions shape the day like a potter molds clay.

Taking responsibility for your attitude, actions and consequences is the path to adult maturity.

Breaking rules to gain an advantage is a serious, unacceptable violation of fairness in competition.

You can`t be perfect, but you can be honest. Admit your mistakes, apologize and make restitution.

Propaganda: manipulating public perception to appear right. High Character: doing what is right.

Integrity is the personal armor protecting your identity and reputation against slander.

Drug abuse cause and effect: like a mall escalator going up…you see your character going down. A temporary 'drug-high' replaces sacrifice with fantasy, stealing the reward of true achievement.

Gossip cools trust and burns relationships. Running with a rumor is cheating in the race. Resolve issues before issues dissolve you. Violence fades when peacemakers shine.

Ignoring a serious injury is not a sign of courage and toughness…its foolish and dangerous! Injuries can distract the mind and alter your future. Talk to your trainer or doctor for proper care.

Behavior is a witness for wisdom. Are your motives pure? Do you think of others before yourself? Do you demonstrate patience with the elderly and children? Do you extend mercy to others the way you want others to extend mercy to you. Are you tripping over a grudge or walking in grace?

The sun warms the entire world; follow the example of the sun…shine your light on everyone.

Addiction is a cycle of punishing waves eroding the emotional foundation of your maturity. Feeding addiction allows your cravings to eat — a steak to a lion is an appetizer for more meat. Put temptation in a cage and lock the door!

Opening addiction's door once temptation subsides, is inviting temptation back into your life. Stopping temptation in motion is like trying to catch a BIG boulder tumbling into the ocean.

Classic liars rationalize dishonest actions to receive an instant reward they believe they deserve. Liars are cowards: replacing fact with fiction to avoid serious consequences of selfish behavior. Self-deception fakes a noble motive to participate in an evil action for personal satisfaction.

Spying on an author's typing (keylogging) to steal and publish his concepts is dishonest plagiarism. The plagiarist is a fake farmer selling cherries from a tree he did not grow. "Thou Shalt Not Steal."

Practice self-disclosure. Share your heart honestly with a trustworthy and understanding friend. Surround yourself with positive people supporting your goals with prayer and accountability. Honest friends identify your blind spots (hidden flaws) to make your character complete.

Alligator-skin-toughness: embrace constructive criticism; dismiss unsupported opinion. Ignoring a minor insult prevents a major argument from high-jacking your joy and productivity.

Judgmental critics attack their opponents with inaccurate information and painful prejudice. False accusation: your word against their word – your integrity will be your 'character' witness.

Praise positive behavior – confront negative behavior. Be sincere with tact and strong in facts. Setting the 'behavior bar' too high leads to inconsistency, hypocrisy, and perceived favoritism.

Bullies use physical size, group power, and social media to spread lies that destroy innocent lives. Making victims feel bad – makes bullies feel good. Bullies have protectors who blame the victim.

Before sacrificing your 'A-game', ask yourself: *is tonight's pleasure…worth tomorrow's pain?* Truth is like a radio - distance creates deafness. Fools ignore stop signs crashing into BIG trouble. Painful consequences are itchy clothes made from rash decisions.

You and your actions are one in character: divorcing your character allows space for mistakes. The further you move away from the light, the more attractive the darkness becomes. You look for answers in places you should not go.

Major mistake; excusing laziness: *I will water, prune and fertilize my garden tomorrow.* Procrastination is a weed choking-out a need. Responsibility today prevents trouble tomorrow.

Are you an ant or an anteater? Are you self-motivated, hardworking and productive; or a lazy slacker making excuses while feeding-off the energy and effort of teammates pulling your weight?

Did you win the day or snooze it away? Your weak, mediocre work ethic will be your sad legacy. Fear of an obstacle becomes its own obstacle — blocking you from over-coming the first obstacle.

Time is space driven by the breath of God, into the hands of God. Time ticks dreams into reality. Time management is gravity for your goal, keeping you grounded in priority and flow.

Alluring distractions entice thrilling satisfaction. Foolish pleasure blurs vision for sacred treasure. Selfish desire is a bad bargain. Adam traded a garden of fruit trees for a field of rocks and weeds. Like fruit softening in rot — sweet success let`s your guard drop. Avoid foolish, high-risk activities. An ego trip will trip you up. Failure has no scream like crashing hope on the cliffs of dreams.

Negative attitude: an ungrateful, critical, pessimistic view of your experiences or relationships. How do you perceive responsibility? Negative — *No! I don`t want to do this, it`s too much work!* Positive: *Yes! I will commit to this special opportunity to help the team and learn a new skill.* Positive Attitude Word (PAW): Appreciation for sacrifices providing traction for your giftedness.

Are your actions on the same team as your goals? Violating rules disrupts flow, stinging the soul. Opening seductive doors: be honest about temptation - curiosity stimulates regretful behavior. Lock-out pesky mosquitos: little images become BIG distractions buzzing inside your head. Wild passion is like a zoo without barriers — pleasure becomes sharp pain in the food chain. Desire drives reckless thoughts. Thoughts are vulnerable vehicles for rolling passion into action. Stopping the motion of unchecked emotion: before you go too far - apply the brakes on the car.

Avoid arrogant people who disrespect authority - believing their actions are above the rule of law. Trust and a lie cannot live in the same room — it's like eating soup with a hole in the spoon.

Losers cheat to win: they lack the character and courage to honor rules and compete fairly. Issuing yourself a license to cheat, drives your body-of-work down a dead-end street.

Steroids in sports are thieves; stealing your integrity and your opponent`s hard fought victory. Steroids pump-up muscles and deflate reputation. Your legacy as a leader will change to cheater.

Planted firmly in the deep soil of character, a team of trees stand tall as a protective wall. Character is capital for future career investments. High Character wins top jobs!

High Character Inspires Boldness For Battle!

Noble Thoughts Have No Boundaries

Rules are boundaries - boundaries keep you safe.

Safe from hurting yourself - safe from hurting others.

Leaders treat players with respect - respect honors leadership.

Leadership expects cooperation – cooperation is not a feeling...cooperation is a fact.

Facts guide wise choices – fiction influences foolish choices.

Foolish choices have consequences – consequences discipline and train.

Training develops High Character - High Character produces noble thoughts.

Noble thoughts have no boundaries.

Lean, Clean, Character Dream

Run the stairs to your dreams on efficient, 'light-footed' character. Carrying suitcases loaded with selfish, regretful actions is a 'heavy-footed' burden. Don`t sabotage goals with reckless choices. Deaths from drugs, car accidents, and senseless murders shock and destroy families.

Obey God`s word—Honor your parents—Save sex for marriage—Learn to earn and manage money. Trusting God with possible, future, financial set-backs liberates the mind for today`s hard work.

Performance Parables

Sunset & Sadness

The old man inhaled the spunky spring air attempting to walk-off the rich calories of his delicious, ham and fried potatoes dinner. Looking up into the evening sky, he saw a spectacular, majestic, gray and salmon angel with air-brushed feathered wings. Inspired, the old man searched for someone to share in his moment. He looked up and the brilliant angel had melted into the night. Embrace opportunity before it fades away.

Technique or Toughness?

After a BIG breakfast, the rancher informed his two sons, Buck and Billy, they would be cutting down the dead oak tree at the end of the driveway. *Buck, fetch the chainsaw, and Billy, you bring the gloves,* the father emphatically directed. Billy, quickly told on Buck for breaking the chainsaw. Buck replied, *I asked you to take the chainsaw to the shop on your way to town, but you said, no!* The father instructed his sons on how to chop down the tree with an axe. Buck attacked the tree with explosive force, but his wild cuts made minimum impact. Billy focused and swung the axe correctly, but quit after a few minutes. Selfishly, they blamed each other for their own failure. Buck`s lack of technique prevented the consistent angles required to chop down the oak tree. Billy`s precision lacked the toughness for completing the task. Skill & Strength are one team!

Value Your Opportunity To Shine!

David`s High Character

Service: David played calming, comforting music for King Saul`s peace of mind.

Responsibility: David took care of his family`s flock of sheep.

Obedience: David followed his father`s orders to deliver food for his brothers on the battlefield.

Mental toughness: David ignored unfounded criticism accusing him of selfish motives.

Courage to speak up: David called-out Goliath for defying the Army of the Living God.

Loyalty: David would not let Saul`s jealousy divide his friendship with Jonathon (Saul`s son).

Strong, noble leadership: David was a popular, victorious general and a wise, respected king.

Repentance: David`s weakness (inclination) for lust resulted in sin (disobeying God`s word). God convicted David of his adultery, deceit, and murder. After wrestling with his agonizing guilt, David confessed his disobedient acts; receiving forgiveness and a restored relationship with God.

Inspirational: "Man after God`s own heart." David lived faithfully and fearlessly in God`s presence. He experienced and expressed God`s Word with poetic genius. David`s intimate, passionate worship revealed his deep, unique relationship with God. David loved God with all of his heart! Sadly, the final chapters of David`s kingship eroded into disobedience and disappointment.

Greek philosophers taught the path to virtue and happiness was through self-help principles, positivity, and discipline. But God infuses His strength into your weaknesses with noble traits. Love vs hate. Patience vs anger. Humility vs pride. Optimism vs negativity. Good-will vs jealousy. Unity vs trouble-making. Thoughtfulness vs self-centeredness. Contentment vs greed/coveting. Thankfulness vs complaining. Confidentiality vs hurtful gossip. Gentleness vs harsh words. Good vs evil. Respect vs bullying. Honesty vs lying. Honor vs cheating. Loyalty vs unfaithfulness.

Fellowshipping with God in spontaneous prayer, authentic worship, and relevant Bible teaching fills your heart with His love and purity, prompting you to reach out and help neighbors in need. Daily, commit your character weakness to God. Quote scripture at temptation, pray and move into God`s presence with sincerity and faith. He may surprise you with a new, noble passion!

A Pure Heart Inspires Noble Actions!

Step Four: Winning Practice Principles

Activity Management

Warrior Circle of Performance Vitality

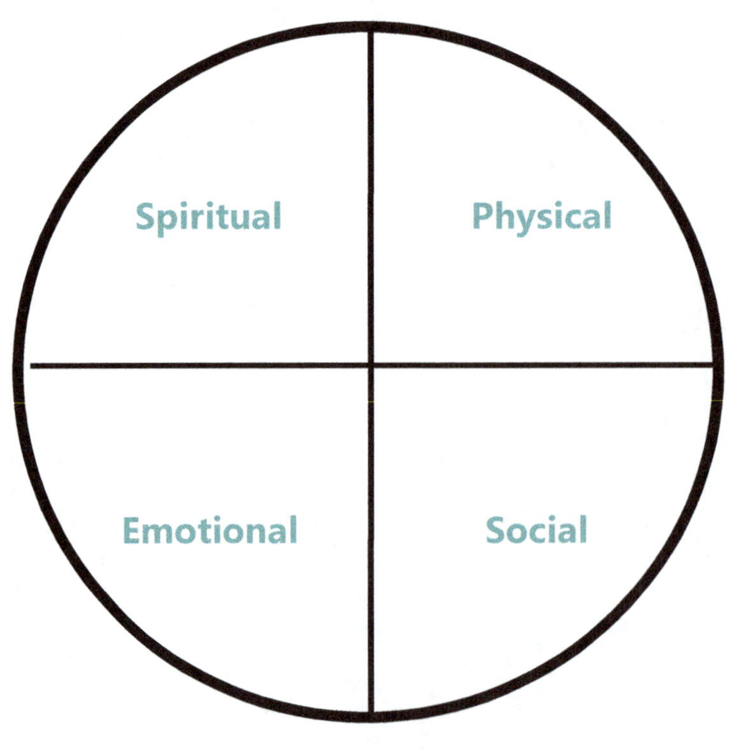

Practice Patience in Progression

Crops are not micro-waved; they are grown. Skill requires patience in process and progression. Young farmers persist in hard times of trials/adversity; perceiving setbacks as on-the-job-training. Failure is fertilizer for new growth. Mistakes are learning steps generating needed improvement. Boney branches flex buds in spring, lifting the glory of summer's green.

Learning a new skill is like putting a puzzle together. Learning each step of the skill fits another piece into the puzzle until the picture is clear/complete. Competition binds the pieces together. Testing your skill against advanced players is the best practice for your performance development.

First priority: *Am I working harder than my opponent to master the skills required to finish first?* Cunning opponents should motivate a burning sense of resolve, focus/purpose in your work-outs. Fork-in-the-road decision: the left, low road is easy with minimum effort/minimum growth. The right, high road is hard with maximum effort/maximum growth. Which path will you choose? Rock climbing school: study, sacrifice, struggle and succeed in mastering your mountain-top goal.

Don't shrink back from your competitor's explosiveness. Use your intangibles to counter size/ strength. Impact the game with your Special Skill. Be aggressive - outhustle your opponent! Athletes who love to compete, take advantage of opportunities to make game-changing plays. Championships are often won by less athletic, but higher-skilled/well-prepared attacking teams. God is not restricted by small forces – God is restricted by small faith. Do not doubt...trust God! Underdogs long to prove critics wrong. David took a risk and defeated a giant!

Grow strong in your skill. Seasons may set with the sun, but mastering your craft has just begun. You are either stepping-up to improvement today, or falling into a hole of mediocrity tomorrow. Performance demands investment and assessment. Egotistical players look out of their performance jar clouded with euphoric, self-praising assessment of their success and popularity. Objective coaches look into a clear jar, identifying flaws/weaknesses and a mediocre work ethic. Do not settle in your strength: if you don't address your weakness - your opponent will.

Win your practice: be eager to learn! Master your role/giftedness for certainty and competency. Take advantage of teambuilding activities that unite/ignite motivation and effort for excellence. Maintain a progress journal. Review takeaways from previous practices, identify today's goal. Productive practices reward organized, transparent coaches who apply discipline consistently. Each mastery of skill is a step-up the success ladder – a higher view inspires you!

Think of improvement as sculpture: practice and competition carving out your performance. Correcting one mechanical flaw in practice can transform your Special Skill into game success. Poor player execution at the end of the game, erases great team execution during the game. Perfecting your dream during the season prevents a nightmare in the post season.

Protect Peaceful Focus: honor rules, watch your words, make wise choices, meet responsibilities. Players or people who feel unfairly wronged by your speech/actions can resort to false accusation. Fools smell smoke and ignore fire. Resolving issues in the present, prevents revenge in the future.

The endurance factor: strength/conditioning provide energy/stamina for the game and overtime. Stamina provides a stronger and longer practice. Muscles make a difference; train for power. Trainers design work-outs for flexibility, footwork, balance, reflexes, agility and explosive jumping. 100% commitment: discipline and diligence destroy space for procrastination and laziness. Fatigue impairs reflexes/reaction time in performance. Endurance provides knock-out firepower! Winners are energetic, stronger and more competitive at the end of game than their opponents.

In stressful, high-expectation performance, fitness/flexibility are wise investments in your health. Extreme repetitive movement can damage ligaments and joints. Peaceful Focus relaxes muscles. Constantly overwhelming your body with extremes, will eventually breakdown your health. Train for sprinting (quick-twitch muscle fibers) and distance running (slow-twitch muscle fibers). Basketball lanes open-up in the second half (from fatigue) for fast lay-ups and run-away victory!

Tough, demanding practice competition replicates intense game speed, pressure, and fatigue. Effective coaches call-out mistakes, demonstrate solutions, and praise player/team success. Coaching cowardice: deflecting game failure onto your unprepared team for new situations. Never discipline a player in the game, if you have not demonstrated the technique in practice. Fairness in leadership matters, consistency in consequences creates credibility for coaches. Players respect coaches who award playing time on merit not on the politics of pleasing donors.

Game readiness requires visualizing and role-playing surprise adversity, special plays for specific situations, time-management, inclement weather, hostile environments/communication issues. The golf course can be a cruel monster of intimidating obstacles producing doubt and confusion. Peaceful Focus advantage: visualize your target, relax-focus and swing through the ball with belief. Smooth, steady efficiency in connecting shots to the green eliminates desperation for heroic play. Round 1 - establish rhythm. Round 2 - master the course. Round 3 - score low for high confidence. Round 4 - finish strong! Attack the course with reasonable risk for efficient par and birdie reward. Playoff strong: stay optimistic in the moment; trust your putting plan, finesse flows out of peace.

Winning is a party in the brain - where ego shines brighter than the game. Winning blinds weakness; blind spots become glaring targets in BIG games. Improve every week...aim for the playoffs to peak. Complete performance is a long, searching river of trials, surprise and survival. Bike riding starts with falling-off the bike in pain; mistakes cause pain that produce change. Your worst problem can be your best teacher; learn the lesson in your trial. Trust God for wisdom.

Preparation creates readiness for assignments. Assignments identify responsibilities for response. Response becomes automatic in repetition. Repetition preps answers for the competitive test. Pass the test...WIN!

Winners Do What Winning Requires!

Grow Your Brain – Grow Your Game

Learning is birthed in curiosity to understand life. Knowledge is the blueprint for building skill. Knowledge, skill, and ability: Study – Practice – Compete – Evaluate – Improve – Hit The Target! Converse in your craft: learn the terms and history of your sport; coaches respect due diligence.

Knowledge prepares adjustments and empowers special tactics for weapons on the battlefield. Military experts travel to distant countries to research culture, terrain and weather conditions. Study all factors of the game venue to prepare for surprise challenges disrupting your strategy.

'Snap-shot' recognition: intense, focused identification of a picture, pattern, number or action. Focused hitters in baseball 'photograph' the ball out of the pitcher's hand to identify a strike. Practice memory skills: police officers can describe specific details of a suspect's appearance. Tip: mentally, picture the object that you are searching for; imagine a face to remember a name. Take a drive in the country and identify unique objects; the next day 'replay' your mental video.

Guided experience builds-out the 'learning center' in your brain; providing belief for new tasks. Volunteering discovers natural abilities, identity, leadership, teamwork and career choices. Mastering the new idea: receive info, discuss, apply, correct, repeat steps; understand new idea. New ideas network information into concepts (Warrior Winning Plan) that improve performance. The unknown (abstract) is married to the known (concrete) by connecting new ideas to pictures. Most fundamentals start in the ready-balanced position; feet (shoulder-width apart), knees bent. Study film of fundamentals, observe demonstration and connect basic steps to the ready position.

Recognition and recall retrieve familiar information. Repetition memorizes vocabulary words. Reading recognizes words describing experience in action. Books build belief for self-expression. Imagination enlightens the mind, like lightening cracking open the sky. Parables paint life lessons. Use the Warrior Winning Plan in personal time-management systems to create time for reflection.

Study documentaries of visionary leaders, generals, historical pioneers, and persistent inventors. Reading and absorbing the adventures of David overcoming impossibility with God's possibility emboldens a daring, adventurous spirit in you. David's poetry inspires insights of God's care.

Being certain in knowing how to perform a skill inspires confidence to master a higher skill. Knowledge and confidence provide the powerful partnership for developing your Special Skill. Ignorance tethers potential. Sharpen your performance pencil - knowledge in…new skills out!

Brainstorming: discussing and connecting new ideas illuminates a more articulate, insightful idea. Team-brain advantage: all members communicating team philosophy/principles in competition. The team communicates needs to the brain - the brain responds to meet the needs. Team brain: softball infielders prevent errors by cooperating with the outfielder's communication on fly balls.

Productive practice starts with innovative ideas producing excitement for mastering new skills. Elementary volleyball situational practice: serve volleyballs to hula hoop targets on the court. Stretch a line of flags along the top of the volleyball net as a visual to prevent serves into the net.

Don`t let yesterday`s glory blind today`s innovation - surf a space-time wave into a new trend. What the heart believes, the mind sees as possibility. Dreams drive goals to glory.

Knowledge Is Only As Good As The Action It Produces!

Athletic Animal Approach

C.A.T.
Commit your performance to God.
Ask for wisdom. **T**rust for success.

Lion Linebacker
Speed and agility with take-down ability.

Rhino Blocker
Explosive attack knocking opponents back.

Monkey-Move Groove
Smooth, rhythmic flow for elite control.

Eagle-Eye Execution
Quick perception for surprise connection.

Alligator Deception
Disguise to strike with a bite.

Fetch Readiness "Good Dog!"
Blast-off efficiency securing a moving object.

Horsepower-Kick
Finishing the race with that extra gear!

Jungle Competition: Eat or Be Eaten!

Persistence – Mental Strength
Grinding through hardships, hunting for success.

Readiness – Alert Response
Anticipation to attack the game in front of you.

Bravery – Toughness to Get It Done
Cowardice fumbles opportunity.
Courage executes opportunity.

Reward – Victory Dinner!
A hungry 'pride' devouring a delicious prize.

Most athletes understand and respond to animal examples for executing approach in special skill. Examples: *focus like an eagle, run like a racehorse, tackle like a lion, block like a rhino, go get the ball like a dog fetching a frisbee, swing through the rings like a monkey swinging through the trees.* Competitors relate to animal, action adventures!

Athletic Attack Innovation!

3DFLASH ATTACK Basketball – Downhill Advantage-SPRINT!

3DFLASH ATTACK (3DFA) Principles: Overload the court (strong side); clear space…run thru the key; screen and pass to flasher at low post, wing or elbow; **Drive…**attack the key, **Draw** the double team and **Dish** to roller or weak-side cutter to finish or make the extra pass. Driver can score off-the-dribble. Utilize both sides of the court. Start actions from multiple entry points. Opportunities open-up with surprise cuts/pin-point passing in the paint. Cutter plays: dive, angle, give-n-go, front, fill, Ghost, slice, curl, baseline and back door. Play through contact in finishing lay-ups! Utilize the opposite-side of the rim to prevent open lay-ups from being blocked from behind. Screen plays to shooting space: curl, stagger, double, down, slip, corner pin, flare, and bump.

Open shots flowing out of 3DFA allow players to step into their shot with confidence and rhythm. Opponents (behind in the score) tighten-up and miss shots. Do not complicate winning; making uncontested shots while your opponent misses contested shots produces winning basketball!

No pain in the lane: drive the ball into the key, jump stop and draw the double team (do not force a shot or commit a foul); shot fake, finish, or kick. 3DFA unpredictability: multiple offensive options. Inside-out passing to perimeter shooters makes opponents pay for packing-the-paint. Fast vs Forced: 3DFA does not rush or force shots; patient, organized offense is the priority.

Quick (shot) recognition enables hustling Rebound Hounds to anticipate and attack the boards. Rebounders beat opponents to the block, board, ball (opposite side of shot) for put-backs. Leaders Lead - Passers Pass – Drivers Drive - Shooters Shoot – Rebounders Rebound – Bigs Battle! 3DFA: creative, skilled teammates playing well together in finding ways to win.

Vertigo Handles: creating shots off-the-dribble takes advantage of mismatches, uncontested jump shots, fatigue, open lanes, and free throws for high percentage tactics to close-out games. Success at the rim: vision, angle, explosiveness, speed, strength, balance, instincts, moves (either hand), and toughness to finish lay-ups. *Rack it!*

Disciplined defense disrupts offense by Taking Away Space and lanes with active hands and matching footwork to stop the dribble-drive. Stay down on shot fakes! Do not gamble on steals! Memorize hesitation-crossover moves, anticipate passing patterns for turn-overs and transition. Be unpredictable in pressuring the ball; trap at the mid-court, sidelines, corners and the key. Assign your center to call-out plays, drives, skip passes, kicks and uncontested sharp shooters. Fast recognition communicates organized rotations for quick-help-recover and smart charges. Alert defenders settle-in to communicate, seal-off the key and make 'tough shots'…tougher. Subjective referees allowing illegal (over-aggressive) contact create hostile situations for players.

Spy-Deny Press: surprise, aggressive, full-court deny press in the second-half (after free throws). Inbound defender hustles to trap and lock down entry pass into the corner; opposite defender rotates and denies pass back to inbound passer. Half court press defenders (alert to the pass over the top of the press) yell-out location of inbound pass (left or right); deny funnel pass or intercept pass out of the trapped corner. Press objectives: deny pass back to inbound defender; commit 100% to legal traps; visualize, anticipate and shut down passing lanes without reckless fouling. Fast rotations for total, court lockdown produces turnovers. Sprint back when press is broken.

Apply 3/4 court press with discretion. Focus on establishing the rhythm of 3DFLASH ATTACK.

Organized early offense: quick-hitter plays before the defense gets back to set up (SPRINT!). Pass ahead to tall, fast wings attacking mismatches for easy lay-ups (executed in four seconds). Execute wing give-n-go, wing screen-roll, drag screen or wing pass into the post for dive cut. Hustle reward: look up (do not over-dribble) and pass to the sprinting center open in the key.

Transition tyranny: forcing passes or dribbles into crowded areas produces fouls and turnovers. Quicksand turnover: dribbling between two defenders doubles the disruption of hands/feet. Forcing shots kills momentum. Stay organized and execute 3DFA to create an uncontested shot.

Counter high-pressure paint defense on the inside with BEEFF Sharpshooting on the outside. Creative, pass-first point guards initiate attack. This requires two skilled players for each position. Players afraid of the BIG moment become weak-link liabilities in championship competition. Establish second-half momentum: outhustle/outscore your opponent in the first five minutes.

Smart screen art: legal, effective screens require timing, technique (correct angles) for hard cuts. Overload and start screening action from the weak-side of the court for passing to surprise cutter. One-on-one offense (ISO): attack weak-side space for post play, direct drives and pull-up jumpers.

3DFA against zone defense: screen/attack gaps for options. Drag low-defender to the corner and pass to weak-side cutter. Take open shots at free throw line/corner. Execute high-low pass and center attack. Defenders doubling-teaming attack cannot contest shooters sliding-to-space.

3DFA advantage: organized, creative offense to break down your opponent's pressure defense. Maximum efficiency with minimum turnovers produces more shots for momentum and runs. Keeping the defense off-balance (chasing cutters and passes) induces out-of-position fouling. Balance: multiple players with Special Skills scoring, defending and draining opponent's energy. Bold, fast, creative play exciting the crowd. Smart strategy and surprise for closing the game. Flexible offense to counter multiple defenses. Uncontested shots in BIG moments for the win!

Five important reasons to make your free throws: Free throws = easy points. Your makes/their misses can make the difference in a close game. BEEFF shooters stay in the game at 'crunch time.' Successful free throws prevent fouling to stop the clock. 'Cool' free throws ice-the-win.

Get to the free throw line for bonus points. Approach: minimizing movement prevents mistakes. Isolate the shooting hand for back-spin and control. Utilize a relaxed (soft), release-rotation wrist snap into the 'cookie jar.' Slow down: rushing your routine and shot results in missed free throws. Do not start your routine on-the-line until you are relaxed and ready (Peaceful Focus) to shoot.

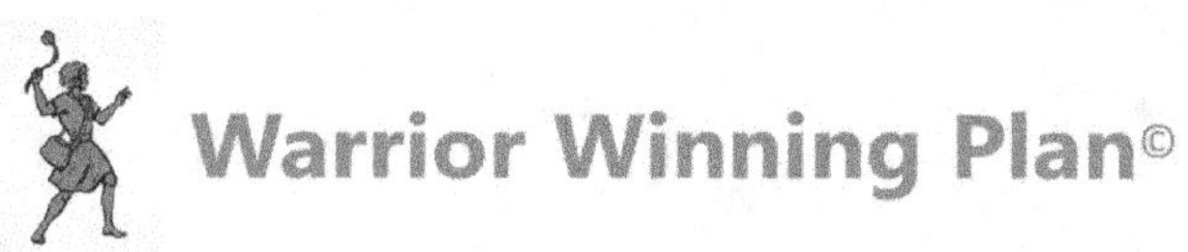

Plant shooting foot towards the hoop: create rhythm; bend your knees and raise up on your toes. Tip: use the off-hand to help balance the ball, but do not incorporate it into the follow-through. One-handed free throws: start 3' in front of the basket - step back 3' and repeat stroke. Practice free throws after sprints. Shoot free throws during scrimmage with reward or penalty. Establish a 5% improvement goal. Improve today...play better tomorrow!

3DFLASH ATTACK Basketball Program

Personable, High Character coach who communicates, motivates and develops all players. Team players with solid fundamentals performing Special Skills at a consistent high-level. 3DFA creating uncontested shots on offense and contested shots on defense for the win! Affordable youth camps developing High Character and Fundamentals into feeder programs. Enthusiastic support from family, fans, athletic director, administration, community and media.

Unpack the Paint: wings cross to opposite sides; center and forward flash three feet outside elbows; guard passes to wing for screen/give-n-go, or passes to center for high-low dive or attack.

For the stunning win! Surprise, sideline out-of-bounds play: overload left side of the half-court; tall, fast athletic wing inbounds the ball; point guard is positioned behind the inbound defender; off-guard sets screen for point guard; center positioned at left elbow; forward at left, low block. Play: point guard cuts off the off-guard's back screen towards the mid-court line as a decoy, forward flashes to opposite wing clearing the key; center flashes to ball and receives the pass; inbound passer cuts inside to the basket for give-n-go pass from the center for an easy lay-up.

For the score! Baseline out-of-bounds plays with passes to screened-shooter, cutter, or screener. Screen curl-cutter to dump. Screen center for lob. Screen inbound passer for flash to space.

Utilize your center's 'triple-threat' skill (pass-dribble-shoot) inside and outside the paint with fluid, instinctual movement to maximize productivity for strategic, high-percentage scoring. Starting play-action with a pass to the center positioned outside of the paint, creates space inside the paint for passing, lobs, screens, cutting, or a direct drive to the hoop. *Rack it!*

Pass into the post with footwork, shot fakes and counter moves for finishing with either hand. Pass to post-trailer for open shot or surprise lay-up. Pick-n-roll priority: pass to roller for attack. Screen the wing for paint attack; center pins his defender creating an open lane to the basket. Quick hitters: release cut, back screen, down screen, pin, high-low, high post shot or spin move. BIG BEEFF Sharpshooters score on pick-n-pop, uncontested perimeter shots and mid-range shots.

Attack 3/4 court press: fast-pass to forward in the corner, drive, draw and lob to center for dunk. Be strong with ball...FINISH!!!

A Skilled Center Is A BIG Scoring Advantage!

The Daring Challenge of 3DFLASH ATTACK!

100% Commitment-Motivation! Warrior strength, toughness and stamina.

Clearing & Attacking Space for locating the ball in a place your opponent cannot defend.

Up-tempo attack initiating your creative style of play for quick points and a great start.

Disciplined defense Attacking/Taking Away Space producing transitions for early offense plays.

Innovative offense for attacking and scoring in the paint; the battle is won in the paint!

No limit for creativity with screens: 'sleight of hand' deception with the screener pretending to hand the ball off, only to drive, draw two defenders and drop the ball off to the low-post.

Multiple entry points for fast actions makes 3DFA hard to prepare for and harder to defend. When the defense knows your offensive patterns, your attack becomes predictable and stalled.

Pass-first point guards directing balanced attack for efficient scoring from uncontested shots.

Screens/cuts and pin-point passing for attackers playing through contact for lay-ups. *Rack it!*

Multiple center positioning for passing, pinning and producing high-percentage shots.

BEEFF Sharpshooters ready to step into their shot with confidence and rhythm.

Savvy, hustling Rebound Hounds anticipating the angle of the ball off-the-rim or backboard. Rebound Hounds control the game and discourage opponents with putback scores.

3DFA takes advantage of scoring opportunities with out-of-bounds plays (sideline or baseline).

Spy-deny Press = turnovers and quick scores.

Faithful, resilient 3DFA system for weathering the storm of your opponent's comeback.

3DFA is fun, winning basketball that attracts High Character athletes to your program!

3DFLASH ATTACK Is Your Competitive Advantage!

Breakthrough Basketball.Com/Screens

Back Screen (cut…off the screen & receive the pass)
The back screen involves an off-ball player setting a screen behind a teammate's defender. This will often catch the defender unaware and allows the offensive player to cut towards the basket where they can receive the pass and finish with a layup.
a. (4) steps out of the low post and sets a screen on 2's defender.
b. (2) cuts backdoor towards the hoop.
c. (1) passes to 2 for the open layup.

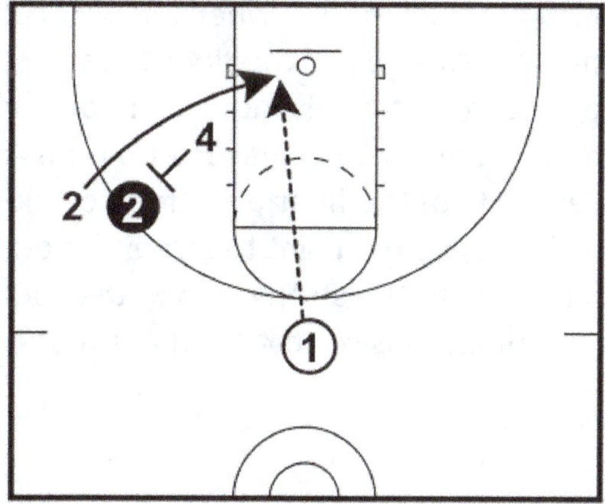

Screens used by permission.

Ball Screen (cut…off the screen & attack the hoop).
A ball screen is a broad term for any basketball screen set for the player in possession of the basketball. A simple tactic to gain an offensive advantage.
a. (4) comes out of the low post to set an on-ball screen on 1's defender.
b. (1) uses the screen and attacks the hoop.

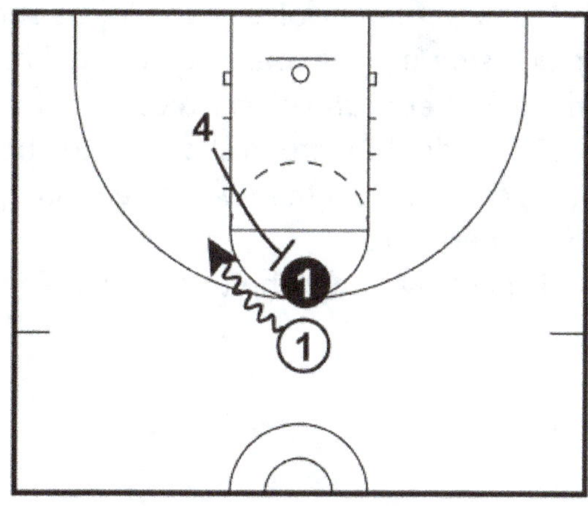

Screens used by permission.

Cross Screen (quick hitter action!)
A cross screen occurs when a player cuts to
the opposite side of the floor to set a screen
for a teammate. This most commonly happens
in the paint, to get a player who is on the
weak side of the floor open for a quick shot.
a. (2) cuts across paint to screen 4's defender.
b. (4) cuts to the strong side of the court.
c. (1) passes inside to 4 for the layup.

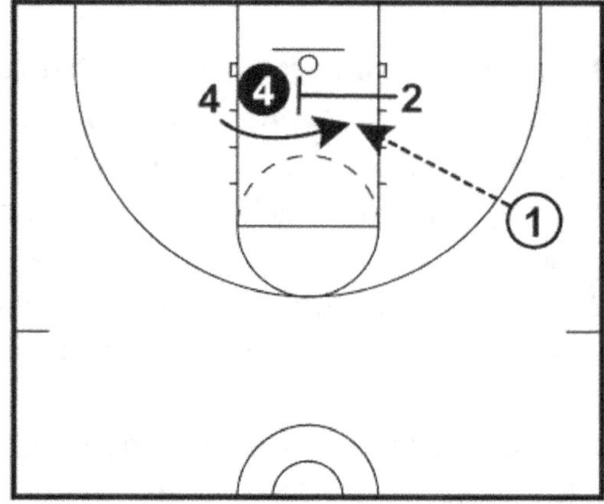

Screens used by permission.

Double Screen (double trouble for defender)
A double screen involves two players setting a
screen side-by-side; making it more difficult for
the defender of the player receiving the screen.
a. (3) & 4 double screen shoulder-to-shoulder.
b. (2) curls around the two screens and pops- out
to the perimeter.
c. (1) passes to 2 for the three-point shot.

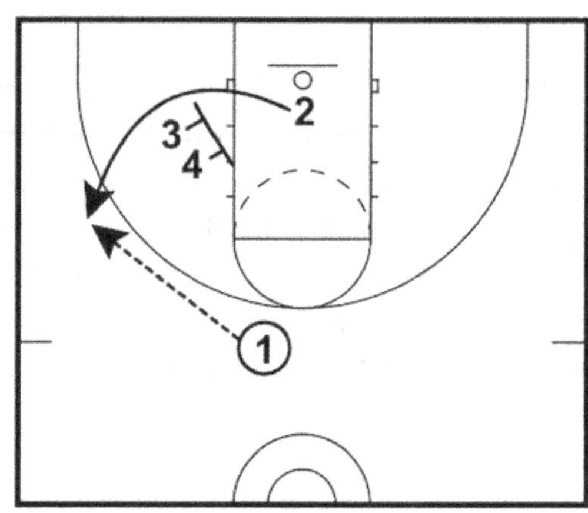

Screens used by permission.

Down Screen (surprise shooting advantage!)
A down screen (also known as a pin down) is any screen that involves the screener facing their chest towards the baseline. The player receiving the screen cuts away from the hoop to get open on the perimeter.
a. (4) steps off the high post and sets a down screen for 2.
b. (2) walks their defender towards the hoop and the explodes out to the perimeter.
c. (1) passes to 2 for the three-point shot.

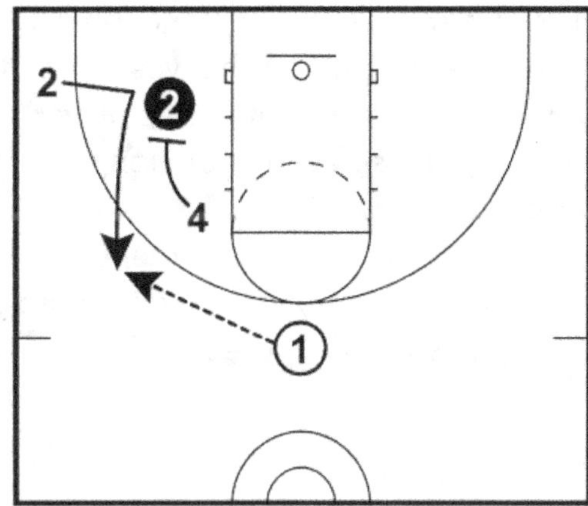

Screens used by permission.

Flare Screen (BEEFF Sharpshooter moving to space)
A flare screen is an off-ball screen that allows a player to cut away from the basketball to a spot somewhere around the perimeter. This is a great basketball screen for getting the team's best shooters open for outside shots.
a. (4) steps out of the low post to set a screen behind 2's defender.
b. (2) cuts from the wing towards the baseline.
c. (1) skip passes to 2 for three-point shot.

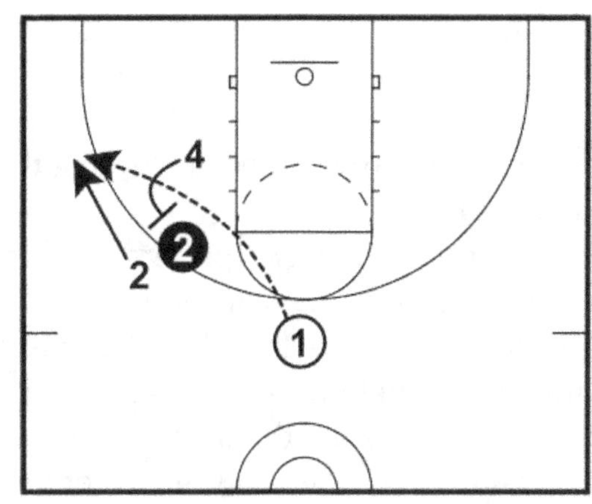

Screens used by permission.

Flex Screen (high percentage lob action)
A flex screen is set on the weak side of the
floor and allows the offensive player
receiving the screen to cut along the
baseline into the paint.
a. (4) sets a screen on 2's defender.
b. (2) cuts along the baseline into the paint.
c. (1) passes to 2 for the layup.

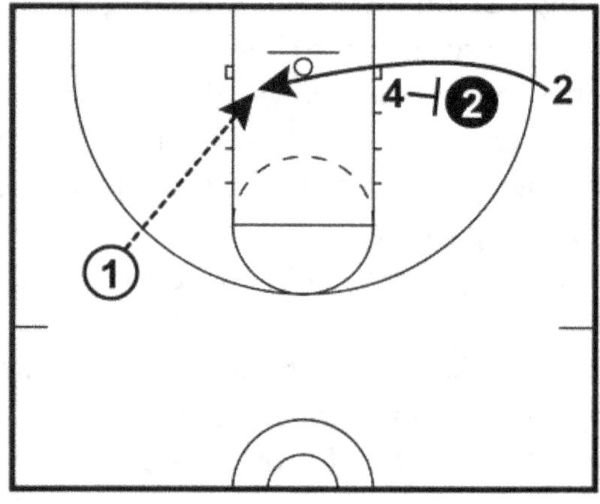

Screens used by permission.

**Horns Screen (two screens blocking the on-ball
defender)**
Horns occurs when two players set a ball screen
on either side of the ball handler's defender.
This happens at the top of the key and gives the
dribbler the option to attack going left or right
depending on what the defense is showing.
a. (4) and (5) step-up and set screens on either
side of 1's defender. (1) reads and attacks hoop.

Flashing-off screens/attacking from all directions
gets your offense into the 'promise land' (paint).

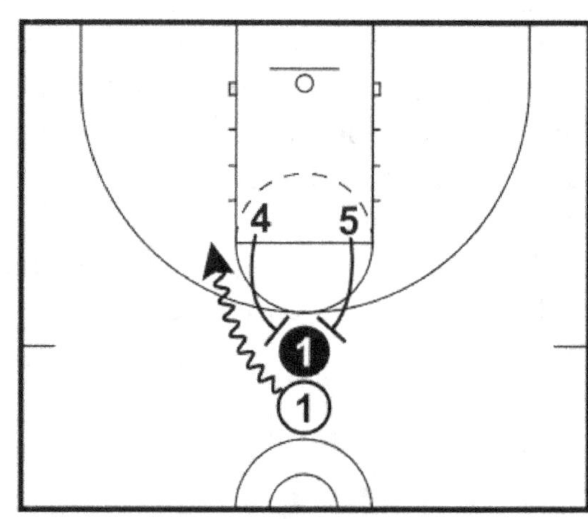

Screens used by permission.

Warrior Winning Plan©

Basketball - BEEF Sharpshooter ©

B 🏀 **Foundation for Fundamentals**

BALANCE Face the basket and set your shooting foot towards the rim. Knees bent in ready position, shoulders squared to the basket. Body vertical over balls of feet, head-up, ball secure in hands.

E 🏀 **Focus On or Above the Rim**

EYES Peaceful Focus: Clear Mind and Confident Heart.

E 🏀 **Line-up the Shot**

ELBOW Elbow, forearm and hand are lined-up directly over the hip, (armpit level).

F 🏀 **Maximize Ball Control**

FINGERTIPS Spread fingertips into the seams of the ball. Cock hand and wrist back. Balance ball with the off-hand; don't incorporate the off-hand into release.

F 🏀 **Release-Rotation Backspin**

FOLLOW-THRU Lift elbow and extend forearm up towards the basket. Snap wrist (backspin) 'into the cookie jar.'

Jim Davis 2022 ©

Attacking Box Volleyball-HIT THE TARGET!

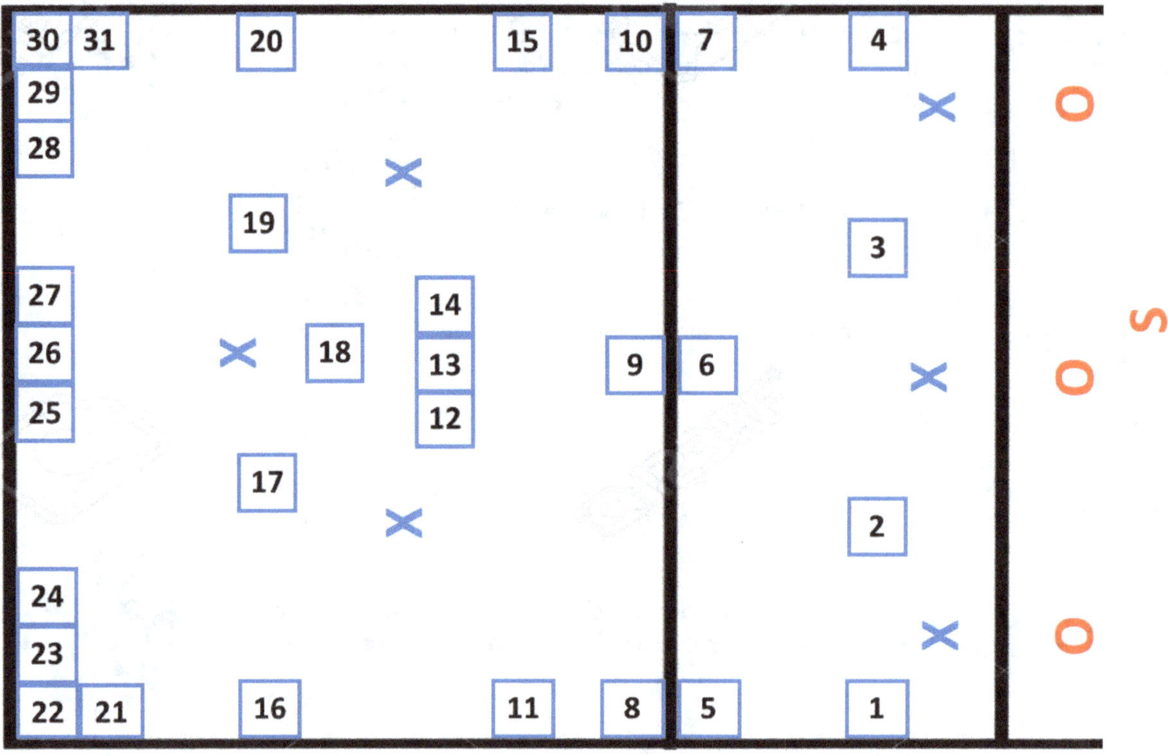

Match smart sets, creative plays, and bold serves to boxes.

Jim Davis 2022 ©

Utilize accurate In-Sync Teamwork to control the ball, Clear & Attack Space and Hit the Target! Keep the defense guessing with creativity – use multiple weapons for attacking the entire court. Set to middle-hitters for quick, sharp angles that limit response time. Tip to boxes with surprise. Unleash explosive, back-row hitters attacking boxes! Take a risk…creative setting wins matches. The setter manipulates the defense, setting-up the hitter to beat-the-block and attack-the-box. Setting skills: deception, timing and placement. Setter scoring: left-handed front dump, right-handed back dump. Matches are won with a fast start and not letting up in dominating the set. Attack weakness with firepower! Stick to the plan and feed the hot hand! Fight and Finish Strong!

Do you possess the Peaceful Focus and skill to execute tough, indefensible serves consistently? Situational serving practice creates precision under pressure. Goal: score three points in a row. Do not rush your serve – trust your approach. Margin of error: serve 3' behind the service line. Serving keys: explosive movement, off-speed, and precision your opponent cannot defend. Serve like a cunning pitcher with sliders and screwballs cutting inside and outside the defender, top-spin fastballs to backline boxes, and knuckleballs that 'die-and-drop' in front of the defender.

Utilize the entire service line, be unpredictable, mix your spots/spin/speed - serve down the line. Visualize your target, relax, jump, focus on the ball and swing through the ball with confidence. Easy serves from you...produce easy points for your opponent. Tough serves to your opponent produce easy points for you. Tough serving stresses defenders - creating scoring runs for you. Low serves just clearing the net limit visibility for recognition/response. Serving wins matches!

'Easy balls' hit to defenders produce quick transition and in-system scoring for opponents. 'Trouble balls' hit away from defenders produce out-of-system (off-the-net play) and free balls. Set free balls to middles for quick scoring. Utilize the setter as a weapon for tip-points to space. Utilize middle-plays to prevent two blockers from Taking Away Space from the outside hitter. Finish shots to boxes with Peaceful Focus and explosive, wrist snap follow-through!

Creative, In-Sync Teamwork controls the ball with precise, passing connections for options. Organized, well-timed plays utilize a 'running advantage' to beat-the-block for explosive spiking! Maximizing physical abilities and mastering spiking techniques accelerates precise, explosive skill. Fast footwork provides time and vision for proper mechanics to pop-up (pass) the ball accurately. Turn 'broken plays' into scoring plays with high-sets to outside-hitters blasting through blockers. Win long rallies with spontaneous team agility in creating/finishing plays anywhere on the court.

A vocal bench inspires starters and energizes fans to create noise and momentum for the team. Depth advantage: train confident, competent subs for specific roles and situations in the match. Use left-handed hitters on the left-side of the net, and right-handed hitters on the right side of the net for natural, efficient swing-angles to cross-court boxes, or straight swings down the line. Utilize roll shots over the block to space. Locate the ball in a place your opponent cannot defend.

Be prepared for your aggressive opponent to start fast with smart attack and explosive firepower. Memorize your opponent's passing patterns for quick-reads and blocking placement advantages. Defense to offense: smart liberos with quick reflexes save balls for their teammates to kill. Effective coaches make adjustments to neutralize their opponent as the match progresses. Leadership, bold blocking, creative setting, and taking advantage of opportunity wins matches!

Assert Your Will With Attacking Box Thrill!

Attacking Box Tennis: HIT THE TARGET!

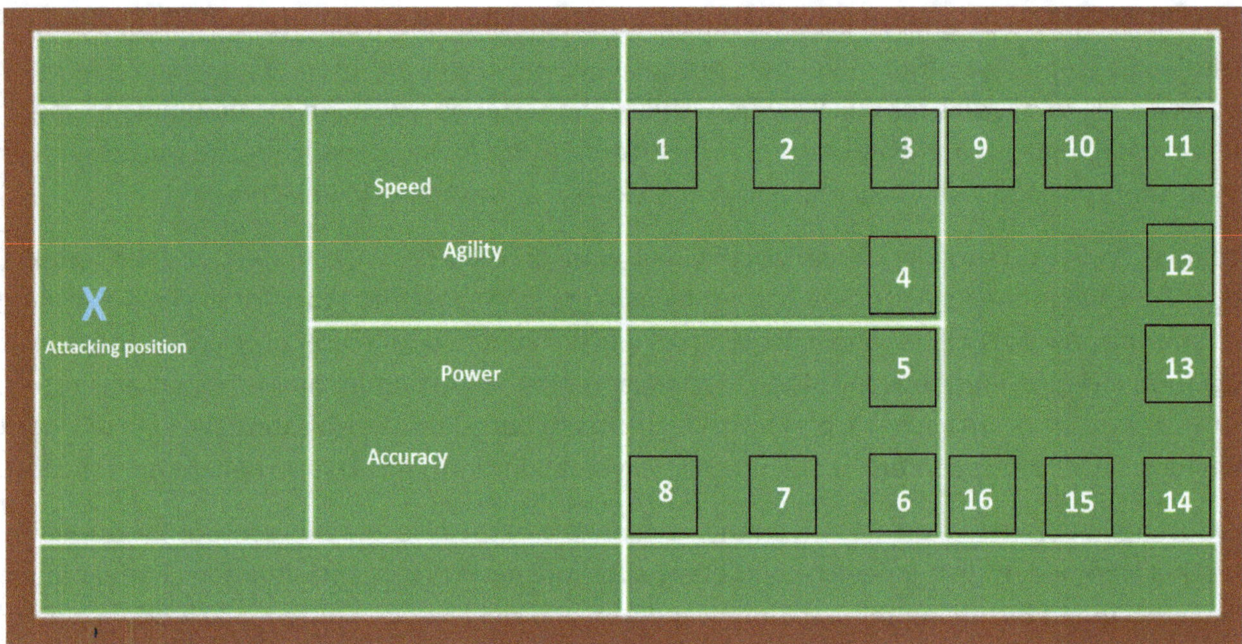

Jim Davis 2022©

Establish Rhythm - Connect Boxes to Open-up the Court - Create and Finish Short Balls

Trust your approach. Clear & Attack Space: play the entire court with boxes/angles for surprise! Set-up winners: move your opponent in all directions. Use variety to create and finish short balls. Be unpredictable/difficult to read: change the pace with off-speed; finish with backhand belief! Memorize locations to start plays. Be smart: pick your opponent apart. Nimble net-play is fun! Push your opponent wide off the court, hustle and cut-off floaters and easy short balls at the net. Finish floaters and short balls with solid fundamentals; don`t rush and get ahead of the moment. Drag your opponent up to the net and pass. Opening-up the court allows you to take advantage of your shot-making skills to lines/space. Be aggressive, take reasonable risks for worthy rewards. Step inside the baseline and hit winners!

- Anticipate patterns. Use fast footwork and balance for stepping into the fundamental. Look up and counter over-anticipation by hitting behind your opponent`s momentum. Disguise drop shots (your opponent cannot defend) when he is playing deep behind the service line or on the run.

- Attack weakness: slow footwork, weak backhand/forehand, poor net play, or lack of power to finish shots. When your opponent is 'back on his heels', keep the ball away from him (unless he is pinned in the corner). Disrupting your opponent`s rhythm/establishing your rhythm separates the score in your favor. Fear of losing sabotages skill and victory. View yourself as a closer. Finish Strong!

- Responsive defense: belief, anticipation, fast reactions, speed, flexibility, agility and racquet control to cover the court. Take Away Space with deep baseline and body shots. Disrupt timing/rhythm with volley, slice, off-speed, and body shots. Defense to offense: redirect rally to the center of the court - use surprise boxes to set-up and finish winners.

First Serve Weapon: easy points, conserves energy, and wins tie breakers. Think like a pitcher.

- Master a simple, fundamentally sound, serving form and rhythm. Establish an offensive serve vs a defensive serve. Easy serves from you, create easy points for your opponent. Tough serves from you, create easy points for you! Visualize your target, relax and focus (do not rush your serve); honor your balance vs rushing and falling forward prematurely.

- The toss is the boss: wait, let the ball drop to the strike zone (contact point) and swing through the ball with confidence. Innovate surprise second serves. Your serve can even the score quickly when you are behind, or become your unstoppable weapon for victory!

- Keep your opponent off-balance: mix spots to boxes, T, and body with ball movement and change of speed. Kick-serve wide to returner stationed deep behind the baseline and volley to indefensible space/box. Volley with discretion: avoid high-risk, attack mistakes; make sure your opponent is on the run and cannot return a ball you are unable to defend.

Return of Serve Identity: not intimidated by power, anticipates patterns, returns with depth.

- Step into your ready position in-sync with the toss; 'photograph' the ball off your opponent`s racquet; start your swing in rhythm with the server`s motion. Attack soft serves! Be wise in break opportunities; you have the advantage…do not force scoring. Returning your opponent`s serve deep to his feet, neutralizes his scoring opportunity; surprising and disrupting his position and rhythm allows you to take control of the rally. Scoring on your opponent`s serve in a tie-break puts pressures him and relaxes you.

Think 'inside the box': collaborate with your coach - design box plays that match your style.

Attacking Box Tennis pressures opponents into mistakes; take advantage of your opportunity. Court management is the key to success - use your mind to keep him on his heels!

Crack The Tennis Code With Attacking Box Approach!

Softball Hitting Success – Warrior Max-swing!

Knowledge provides opportunity to execute skill successfully. Connecting your swing to an explosive rise ball or an off-speed pitch is difficult. A winning approach is imperative when you step into the batter's box - Warrior Max-swing! Timing: get in rhythm with the pitcher's motion. Lift stride foot four inches off the ground as the pitcher raises her arm into the vertical position. Pitch identification (key): photograph the ball out of the pitcher's hand to identify a hittable pitch. Let your stride foot land intuitively as the pitcher delivers the ball. Flexible swing adjustment: adjust your hands to the pitch location. Goal: hitter advantage - anticipation for a hittable pitch.

Your mindset: Peaceful Focus – 100% attention on the ball and readiness to execute your plan (what pitch to take and what pitch you want to attack); posture – head still and body balanced. Warrior Max-swing review: timing, pitch identification, swing adjustment to the pitch location.

The eyes are an extension of your brain, receiving and transmitting information for identification. Trust your eyes to photograph the ball out of the pitcher's hand for pitch recognition: drop, curve, drop-curve, 'backdoor' curve, screwball, rise ball, curve-rise ball, change-up and change-up drop.

Collaborate with your hitting coach - study videos of the opposing pitcher's ball-grip and spin. How will she attack your bat speed or plate coverage? What pitch does she leave over the plate? Which sequence does she utilize to get ahead in the count, even the count, set-up her out-pitch? Does she throw under-the-zone, over-the-zone, inside/outside-the-zone to finish-off the hitter? Preparation produces patterns for recognizing hittable pitches, solid-contact and success!

Common hitting mistakes. Over-play: pulling the outside pitch (swinging over-the-ball), tightening-up and dropping your hands under the ball for an out. Guessing: not identifying a hittable pitch. Bad decisions: swinging at a pitch out-of-the-zone, or taking a third strike with two outs with a runner in scoring position. Getting jammed: over-aggressive swinging in RBI situations. Poor timing: a consistent late swing resulting in a foul ball. Hitting mistakes result in missed opportunities to make solid contact with a hittable pitch. Hitting top pitchers requires taking advantage of pitches hanging over-the-plate. A hitting mistake creates pitcher success.

Stay alert for pitcher fatigue. A tired arm lacks control, speed, and movement; falling behind in the count. Be smart: keep the pressure on a wild pitcher, make her throw you a hittable pitch. Your decisions in the box determine your hitting success. Bad pitches produce bad swings. Disciplined hitters don't pull low-outside pitches, they drive outside pitches to the opposite field. Do not let over-aggression 'trigger' your swing; patience and identification produce base hits.

The anatomy of an error. Mental: disconnected from the play; bad judgement/decision. Distraction: lack of focus to perceive the play. Doubt: lack of conviction to commit to the play. Physical: poor execution attempting to make the play. Pressure: rushing execution (getting ahead of the moment) to make a close play. Panic: fear of failure causing a game-changing mistake. Great plays percolate deep in the soul with strong belief to 'go-get' the ball!

Offense objective: move runner to third base with less than two outs for high-percentage scoring. Example: single, bunt, ground ball placed away from fielder, sacrifice fly, error, passed ball, balk. The cunning pitcher will appeal to greedy, first-pitch swinging in RBI situations. Keep your RBI approach humble, simple and effective: outside pitch-opposite field; middle pitch-center field, and inside pitch-left field (right-handed hitter). Line drives = RBIs!

Trust your approach. When you doubt your approach at the plate - you`ve already struck out! Your uncertainty will throw-off your timing, strike identification, and hand/swing adjustment. Hitting slumps can cause frustration, panic and premature changes in your Max-swing approach. Study video of your present flaw vs your past hitting success – compare and correct the mistake.

Fastpitch softball is exciting competition full of drama, defense, BIG hits and comeback victories! The responsibility of the coach is to honor the integrity of the game and mandate legal pitching. Allowing pitchers to crow-hop throws-off the hitter`s timing, shortens the distance to the plate, speeds-up the pitch; making it difficult to identify a strike & adjust the swing. Keep the field level!

Warrior Max-swing – Your Aggression Connection!

Nine Keys to Softball Victory!

- Multiple pitchers getting key outs in BIG moments.

- Fundamentally sound, vocal catcher with a quick release Hitting The Target!

- Alert defense making plays under pressure.

- Slap hitters 'chopping' the ball close to the plate for BIG hop hits.

- Surprise bunts away from fielders, push-bunts between the pitcher and first baseman.

- Smart, daring baserunning.

- Clutch RBI hitting.

- Fierce resolve - comeback mentality.

- Finding ways to win!

You Are Only As Tough As The Adversity You Have Been Through!

27 Reasons to Believe in the Fastball

1. Creates rhythm, control and a consistent release point for a smooth, repeatable motion.

2. High-percentage pitch to attack the plate, get ahead in the count and finish-off the hitter.

3. Limits walks from falling behind in the count and pitching too fine with breaking balls.

4. Fast speed sets-up off-speed, throwing-off the hitter's timing.

5. Blazing speed pressures hitters into premature decisions or guessing.

6. Fastballs dominate (take advantage of) slow bat speed.

7. Maximizes endurance with strong, leg drive delivering energy to the pitching arm.

8. Minimizes injury with less stress on the arm than breaking balls, screwballs and sliders.

9. High fastballs are difficult to bunt – producing easy pop-up outs.

10. Sets-up your pitching plan instead of living or dying with one-or-two predictable pitches.

11. Tethers base stealing: less time for the runner to beat the throw; effective for pick-offs.

12-15. Inside fastballs freeze hitters looking for the pitch away; or expecting a different pitch with two strikes. Induces (jams the hitter) double-play balls.

16. Low fastballs = ground balls. Groundballs are less likely to go for extra bases/home runs. *Low you roll…high you cry!* Groundballs keep infielders alert/ready to make the correct play.

17. Pulling a low-outside fastball results in a weak ground ball.

18. High fastballs (above-the-zone) exploit free-swinging home run hitters.

19-23. High-inside fastballs (on-the-hands) produce weak flyballs, frustrate squeeze plays, and overpower inside-out swings.

24. Over-the-hands, inside fastball is a go-to 'out' (3rd strike) pitch for aggressive pull-hitters.

25. Low-inside fastball (under-the-hands) is a deceptive 'out' pitch for low-ball hitters.

26. Tailing two-seam fastballs exploit lack of plate coverage for left-handed hitters pulling off the pitch. Left-handed hitters pull low-inside fastballs for home runs. Exploit this 'sweet spot' hitting tendency with an inside 'backfoot' fastball under-the-hands, don't miss your spot! Goal: control the plate with smart fastballs for pitcher advantage.

27. Intimidating fear factor: Extra Gear of Greatness for explosive, closer domination!

The Fastball Is The Father Of Your Pitching Family

www.ingramcontent.com/pod-product-compliance
Lightning Source LLC
Chambersburg PA
CBHW082128180726
48291CB00010B/2774